I0604832

Jeanette Elaine Lopez

Crown Me in Silence

Jeanette Elaine Lopez

Jeanette Elaine Lopez

ISBN: 978-1-0882-3849-3

DEDICATION

For my parents,
whose love and strength have helped me overcome
my struggles.
For my husband,
my greatest supporter in all my projects.
And for my children, my miracles. You are my
reasons to keep going.

PROLOGUE

Gravenport was no ordinary city.

Locals say it was created on power and bloodshed. Whispers on where the name came from, the old grave road, where smugglers came and died.

North Gravenport helped build this city.

South Gravenport continued to destroy it.

Somewhere along the railroad tracks, power split, and Leaders were created.

Outsiders see a quiet town on the edge of water and history. But under the Mansions and Neon Lights, Gravenport remembers every lie, every sin.

The Marcano name rules the North. Like Father, like son, as if family secrets were not enough.

On the **South Side**, the shadow of Valentino Costa moves like smoke, a crown tattoo burned into skin, a promise inked in pain and power.

Between them lies a line that was never meant to be broken, drawn in blood and brotherhood, where love and war collide.

And in those quiet moments, when the wind carries the scent of larkspur and danger, the city holds its breath, waiting for their next move.

CHAPTER 1

My name is Victoria Marcano, and there are three things I know for sure:

1. My brother Rellik is the Leader of The Killers and runs the North part of this city.
2. I was never meant to fall in love with Valentino Costa.
3. And once I did, everything began to unravel.

I look up at the clock, watching the second-hand crawl slower than a turtle crossing the street. I can hear the clicking sound with every passing second, click, click, click.

"C'mon, five o'clock," I mumble under my breath.

I glance around the office, peek through the window to make sure no one's pulling in. Then I check the appointment book. Everyone who needed to come in has come and gone.

Good.

I let out a deep breath, then inhale slow and steady. My lungs expand, chest rising as I begin to count inside my head.

"One, two, three, four, five, six, seven..."

And finally, "eight."

I exhale. My shoulders drop with the breath, trying to ease the anxiety that has caused my brain to overthink once again. The weight on my chest alone has given me an uneasy feeling all damn day. I couldn't wait to get out of here. It's Friday, and the boss has me stuck at the car wash. Most days, I can deal, but today, I'm done. Done with working, done with the bullshit side duties, and mainly done with taking orders from my overbearing boss, who is also my older brother, Rellik Marcano.

Sometimes I still can't help but laugh at the fact that my mom let my dad name Rellik. But if you think about it, he definitely knew what he was doing and planning. Thank the Lord, she named me.

Even though he can be a pain in the ass, Rellik has always taken good care of me. Even provided me with work. He's got me working at one of his locations as a "receptionist." Let's be real, this receptionist job is anything but typical.

I handle more than phones and appointments. There's a whole list of off-the-record duties only I'm in charge of, like entertaining "investors." Today has been full of them, some local, some flying in to kiss Rellik's ring. And it's not even the first Friday of the month.

Every week, he changes my location, posting me wherever he needs me the most. This week, Iron Grave Detailing. I swear the only reason I'm here is so he can keep an eye on me as if I'm some flight risk or super fragile. I don't know why, it's not like I'm out chasing danger. And even if I tried, he'd shut that shit down before I could blink.

I guess being the gang leader of the North Side Killers comes with privileges. Kind of like having an army at your beck and call at all times. Or making sure your little sister stays under lock and key.

I sigh, louder this time, heavier. My eyes flick back to the clock.

The second hand hasn't picked up speed.

Click. Click. Click.

"Tori. Hey, Tori, you ready?"

John's voice snaps me out of it.

I jump a little, nerves still buzzing. "Oh, yeah. Sorry."

I must've been daydreaming again. I think that's the only thing that keeps me sane some days. I grab my purse and belongings and follow John quickly toward the SUV parked outside.

John was one of Rellik's drivers, or shall I say, foot soldiers. Every morning, he picked me up, dropped me off, and came back again after closing. It made me feel like Rapunzel locked away in the North Side Tower of auto parts, engine grease, and overpriced air fresheners.

John was friendly and quiet but kept his distance. Still, he was just a foot soldier. A 6'1", 250-pound wall of a man with light brown hair, fair skin, and a scar just under his right eye socket. I asked him once how he got it, but he dodged the question, and I never brought it up again.

Honestly, I always wondered why Rellik made him my driver. John looked like he belonged in some Hollywood bodyguard firm protecting the next big A-list star, not babysitting his boss's little sister. But then again, why would Rellik assign some scrawny recruit to watch me? What if Tori needed help?

"Oh my God," I mutter sarcastically, "the guy across the street just looked at me."

I laugh quietly to myself. This is my Monday through Friday. If I can't joke about it, I'll cry, and it's Friday, so no way I'm letting my anxiety ruin that.

"Hey John, do you think you can drop me off at Rebecca's today?" I ask. "We're going out tonight, and I'm getting ready at her place."

John stiffens, shooting me a glance that almost looks like fear.

"Uh... does Rellik know? Did he say it was okay?" He mumbles, starting to sweat a little, first his brow, then his forehead.

I laugh to ease the tension. "Dude. He's not my dad, and he's not The Godfather. *Calmate*, will you?"

I catch the insult flash across John's face, but he knows better than to say anything. I'm Rellik Marcano's baby sister, and that comes with privileges, like being untouchable, even to the staff.

Still, it's frustrating. I can't remember the last time a guy looked at me without glancing over his shoulder. It's like I carry an invisible "do not touch" sign.

There was this guy I met once at Nova's Books & Curios. He asked for help finding a book, and we ended up talking for almost an hour, everything from fantasy novels to TV shows. He was charming, and for once, I felt *seen* as if I were just a regular girl.

Before he left, he asked if I wanted to grab coffee sometime. I eagerly said yes.

I remember being excited, planning what I'd wear the night before, even playing out how the conversation might go. I got there early. I waited. I smiled every time the door opened.

He never came.

No text. No call. Nothing.

At first, I thought maybe something serious had happened. But then days passed. I tried reaching out, but never received a response. I finally just gave up.

The second time it happened, it hit even harder. It was someone I already knew, this guy from high school who'd reconnected with me through social media. He was sweet. Funny. Said he remembered me as the girl with a book always in her hand and loud opinions. Said he admired that. We talked for days, and then out of nowhere—silence.

I reread my texts, searching for where I went wrong. Did I overshare? Scare him off? But nothing stood out.

It made me question myself in ways I didn't want to

admit. Was I not pretty or skinny enough? Not interesting? Did I seem too desperate?

But the more I thought about it, the more it felt off. Too clean. Too convenient.

And then it clicked.

It had Rellik written all over it.

The way both guys just disappeared, no trace, no closure? That was exactly how my brother operated, silencing threats before they became problems. And in his eyes, men coming around me? That was a problem.

It made me furious. It made me lonely. But more than anything, it made me feel like I wasn't even living my own life.

Like I was just a pawn on a board he controlled.

I never confronted him about it. Why would I? It would just cause an argument. But it's ridiculous, I am in my 20s. What does he plan to do, keep me locked up until I'm old and pruned? Uggh Gross!

To the rest of Rellik's crew, I was *la fruta prohibida*—the forbidden fruit. I always found that ironic, since I didn't exactly fit the mold of the average swimsuit model.

I'm 5'4", full-figured, with long dark brown hair, and hazel eyes just like my brother. Rebecca likes to say I'm the Latina Marilyn Monroe, with a flat stomach, big booty, and a size 14 in jeans. But you wouldn't know it by looking at me, because according to her, "everything's in the right place."

Still, none of that stopped them from calling me what they did. All it meant was that even if they wanted me, or hell, even just wanted to get to know me, they couldn't. It was forbidden. I was someone they couldn't and shouldn't dare get close to. And if they tried? Rellik would make sure there were consequences.

My dad wasn't even this bad.

At this rate, I'd be 45, still single, and still getting ghosted.

Being his sister was bittersweet. I may not be able to do a lot on my own, but I knew I could always count on him. Rellik always took care of me. He meant well. It's been just the two of us since Papi died. But damn, sometimes, he could be a real ass.

He needs to let me live a little.

"John, c'mon, her house is just around the corner," I huff.

"*Ta bueno, ta bueno,*" he mutters. "But at least let me take you, girls, tonight. I can be your DD."

"Fine. Pick us up at ten," I say, fully aware I'd be long gone by then.

I hated lying to John about the pickup time, but I wasn't about to have a spy on my one night of freedom. Usually, he drops me off at my apartment and doesn't ask questions. But tonight, I didn't want to waste time waiting for Rebecca to get me from my place. This way was quicker.

Even if John seemed unsure now, his face twitched with hesitation, as if he felt responsible for not taking me directly home.

He didn't get it. I needed some freedom. Some time to myself.

What he didn't know was that Rellik and I had made a compromise. Well, more like a negotiated truce. I fought tooth and nail for it, but eventually, he agreed. I could have one girls' night a week with Rebecca, no check-ins, no tails, no surveillance.

He only gave me two rules.

First, North Side establishments only. Obviously.

Second, if I ever felt unsafe, I had to call him. No questions asked.

He preferred Friday nights over Saturdays. But that part, he left it up to me.

I decided not to stir the pot and chose to go on most of my outings on Fridays, unless something specific came up.

We were moving slower than usual, and I glanced over at John to make sure he wasn't having a stroke or some medical emergency. He wasn't. But you could tell he was mentally struggling. The guy was driving like the cops were tailing us.

"John, you're not driving Miss Daisy, can you speed up a little, please?"

He immediately snapped out of whatever dilemma was playing tug-of-war in his brain and pressed the gas. Eventually, we pulled into Cinder Point Estate, the neighborhood where Rebecca lives. John parked in front of her two-story red brick house, the one with a lawn that screamed for help and some withered plants near the doorway. If she lived under an HOA, she'd be fined monthly just for the grass.

"Finally," I sighed, practically leaping out of the SUV as if my life depended on it.

As I walked up to Becca's porch, I heard John call out behind me, "I'll be here at ten, remember."

I waved over my shoulder, giving him a quick nod. Message received.

The second I stepped inside, I kicked off my shoes, ready to head upstairs, but froze when I spotted Becca holding out a Tito's and cranberry cocktail in a mismatched glass, complete with a candy cane straw. She handed it to me, with eyes that said, "Drink up."

"Girl, you took forever," she said. "How was chauffeur number one today?"

I groaned. "John's the sweetest, but he feels more like a prison guard. Or worse, my babysitter. I can't even drive myself to work."

"I still can't believe he bought you that car and won't let you use it."

Right? Last August, my brother gifted me the most beautiful Mercedes-Benz S-Class for over $110,000.

I cried when he handed me the keys, literally cried. I was in shock. It was my dream car, nearly to the tee. I say nearly because he got it in black, and I'd always wanted something custom. Gold. Or at the very least, gold trim.

I'd been talking about getting a Benz since I turned fifteen. It took nearly a decade, but I didn't care. I was grateful. I was in awe for days.

Until I realized the truth.

It wasn't for transportation.

It was a trophy, something to show off. Something to look at, not actually use.

 My birthday was over three months ago. And how many times have I driven that beautiful piece of machinery?

Three.

Three fucking times.

Just sitting there in the garage like some museum exhibit. Wasted.

"Ugh, work sucked today. So many people going in and out of the car wash, and on Monday, he's got me working at North Iron Customs.

"The mechanic shop?" Rebecca asked, slightly confused.

Yes, accepting deliveries all damn day," I complained. "But hey, it's Friday. And I am *so* ready to dance it up tonight."

Mind you, I can't dance to save my life. And Becca? Fully aware. But she's never embarrassed to be seen with me out on the dance floor. That's one of the reasons I love her.

Well, maybe not the main reason.

She was there when Papi died, never left my side. I remember my Tia trying to send her home, but Becca stood her ground, said she wasn't leaving until *I* told her to. She knew how close I was to him. Knew I didn't need words, just someone nearby to hold my hand, hold me.

She's like a sister. The dancing thing? Just a bonus.

Becca wanted to pregame while we got ready, but after the last time, I wasn't about to repeat that mistake. I decided to take it easy tonight, baby sips here and there. Especially since I had no intention of sticking around for John to play babysitter. I just wanted one carefree night out with my bestie. No spies. No watchers. No rules.

Well, except the one I was about to break.

South Side. Just for tonight.

Becca knew all about Rellik's rules. And while she didn't ask if I was sure, she didn't need to. Once I made up my mind, there wasn't much she, or anyone, could say to change it.

Still, she couldn't help herself with the passive-aggressive warnings while we were getting dressed.

"So," she said casually, applying lip gloss across her

mouth, "are we going to our usual place tonight? Oh, wait, nope! We're going to the South Side on our *LAST GIRLS NIGHT EVER!*"

Subtlety? Not Becca's strong suit.

I gave her the look. The kind that says snitches get stitches. She raised her hands in mock surrender and spun on her heel, disappearing into her closet for what had to be the third time.

I was already dressed and felt like I'd been ready for hours. I glanced at the digital clock, **9:05 p.m.**

Time was ticking.

John would be here soon.

"Rebecca, hurry up! We need to leave like now," I shouted from the living room.

"I'm hurrying, damn," she called back, her voice muffled by distance. I heard the unmistakable sound of heels being tossed across the room, followed by huffing, puffing, and more chaos.

The clock blinked back at me: **9:21 p.m.**

John was never late. He probably had a countdown on his damn watch.

"Rebecca," I warned, "if you're not ready in five fucking minutes, I'm leaving your ass here!"

"I'm ready, bitch, damn!" she snapped, finally appearing in the doorway.

And, wow. Rebecca was wearing the sluttiest skirt I'd

ever seen. Like, bad-porn-premise level slutty. She looked like she was auditioning for a Johnny Sins episode, 'Nurse tries to get a promotion,' or some shit.

I gave her the most judgmental look in my arsenal.

"What?" she shrugged, completely unbothered. "You said we're going to the South Side. That's where the hottest men are. Do you think this says *I've been bad and need to be punished,'* or more like *I'm a tease, look but don't touch'?"*

I groaned all in one breath. "It says, 'I tried too hard to look hot, which I always do, but this time I really outdid myself, and now my best friend is spiraling because her overprotective brother is going to go nuclear if he finds out.'"

She rolled her eyes. "You could've just said yes."

9:46 p.m., and we were finally in the car.

As we pulled out, I noticed headlights in the distance behind us, a slow, steady crawl, like someone cruising the neighborhood. My stomach flipped.

Was that John?

If it was, how long would he wait before realizing we were gone? Would he knock? Call? Text? And if I didn't answer, would he start searching? Hit up every North Side club? Call Becca?

Call Rellik?

No. No way. He wouldn't risk that. That'd be like digging his own grave.

Still, just in case, I powered my phone off. No calls. No texts. No distractions. I wanted tonight to be mine, just one night when no one could reach me. No one could watch me. No one could control me.

I wanted freedom. I wanted fun. I wanted to flirt.

The thought made me giggle. Actually, squeal. Like a high schooler getting ready for prom.

Maybe tonight, for once, I'd actually feel alive.

But as we crossed the bridge toward the opposite side of town, my nerves started to kick in.

Was I making the right choice? Was putting myself at risk worth it?

The rivals on the South Side were just as bad as Rellik, if not worse. I heard the rumors. What if someone recognized me?

"Fuck it," I muttered, pressing the gas pedal just a little harder. Wherever I go tonight, I'm just a girl named Tori out with her best friend. No connection. No reason to watch me.

"Okay. Decision made," I said under my breath.

Becca gave me a side glance. "Giving yourself a pep talk about whether or not this is a bad idea, huh?"

"Shut it, Becs. We got this."

Ten minutes passed. The city lights blurred past, and I tried to focus on the road, but the knot in my stomach only grew tighter.

I never got anxious going out. But tonight? Of course, tonight was different. There were so many factors, so many unknowns.

Right now, John was probably blowing up my phone, which I turned off on purpose. He is perhaps panicking that I haven't answered. Or worse, maybe he already figured it out. Maybe he was calling Rellik.

Would my brother think I just ditched John? Or would he know, know, that I broke our agreement?

God. This is why I overthink everything. Why do I dwell?

Just like I did the first time I was ghosted.

Another ten minutes passed before we officially hit the South Side.

The ride to the South Side felt like a countdown. I didn't want to reach zero. Every streetlight we passed was like a checkpoint I couldn't undo. Rebecca chatted about some new guy she met at the gym, but I couldn't focus. My stomach was doing somersaults; it was like butterflies were gnawing at my stomach lining.

"What if he finds out?" I finally blurted.

Rebecca looked over, confused. "Rellik?"

I nodded.

"Girl, you're being dramatic. He's not psychic. He's not going to know unless you call him crying the second we park."

I wanted to believe her. I really did. But something about tonight didn't feel right. I had spent so long following rules I didn't agree with that it was hard even to recognize the sound of my own choices. And now, I was actively breaking the biggest one.

"I just, I hate lying to him," I admitted, staring out the window. "Even if he doesn't deserve the truth."

Rebecca scoffed. "Oh, please, since when has he ever given you the truth?"

I didn't respond. She had a point, but hearing it out loud made my chest tighten.

We passed the last gas station before the South Side border. I always saw it as the line between 'okay' and 'dangerous'. We passed the railroad tracks, the official marker. The shops changed, and the sidewalks were cracked. The cars were older, the faces unfamiliar. It was like stepping into a parallel universe, one where I didn't belong.

But I didn't back down.

Rebecca turned the volume up and glanced at me again. "You, okay?"

"No," I admitted. "I have never broken one of his rules, but let's keep going."

It felt like an eternity.

The difference was immediate. The streets here needed paving; cracks and potholes were everywhere. The vibe was heavier, grittier. Some might say darker. You could practically feel the weight in the air. King runners lingered on corners throughout downtown, flashing hand signs and eyeing traffic. That's when the reality of it all sank in.

Did I really just put myself in danger just to get away from my brother and his crew?

"It's okay. Almost nobody knows you here. Just blend in," I whispered to myself.

Rebecca turned at the same time, giving me a look that screamed, "Are we seriously doing this?"

I took a deep breath and scanned the block to decide where to go first. That's when Becca pointed, of course, to none other than **La Corona**.

I hesitated. Everyone knew La Corona was a King hotspot, and Rebecca definitely knew that. But maybe, maybe nobody would recognize me. Perhaps I'd be another girl on a Friday night.

"Okay, girl. Let's do this," I said, biting the bullet.

I inhaled slowly as we approached the front door. The bouncer barely glanced at my ID, which was probably for the best; my North Side address would've raised eyebrows. Fuck, what am I thinking? My last name alone would have made him sound the alarm.

The club was surprisingly high-class for the South Side. White polished floors. No stench of old beer or cigarette smoke. Even the fog machine was on low. I scanned the room. The bar was clear. Dance floor, clear. VIP, too dark to make anything out.

A wave of relief hit me like a shot of tequila.

"Let's take a shot!" Rebecca shrieked.

I gave her a look. "I'm not carrying your ass to the car tonight."

She rolled her eyes, huffing. "C'mon, biatch. Live a little. We're on the other side of town. Nobody knows you here."

"Fine," I gave in.

We ordered a Purple Gecko, like we used to back in the day. It always gave us the perfect kick to start the night. We used to do Royal Fucks until one god-awful hangover ruined it forever.

As soon as I placed my empty shot glass back on the bar, that feeling hit me. The one that coils in your spine and tightens your shoulders.

Was I being watched?

Or was I just being paranoid again?

I didn't move a muscle; I let my eyes do the work. First left. Then right.

Gotcha.

A guy stood off to the far left of the bar, leaning on the counter and staring dead at us. More specifically, at me. He smiled like he knew something, as if he knew me.

"Becs," I whispered, "look over my shoulder. Do you know that guy?"

"Who?" she asked, loudly. Loud enough that people in New York probably heard her.

I slapped my forehead. "Girl, whisper!" I muttered through clenched teeth. "The one in the corner. Dark, murderous eyes, slightly overgrown nose."

The guy was tall, easily over six feet, with thick, expressive eyebrows and a little wave to his grown-out hair. There was something about the way he looked at me, like he was peeling back a layer I didn't even know I had. He was smiling, but it wasn't friendly.

It was calculated.

It was familiar.

I couldn't place him.

Becca squinted, then scoffed. "Ew. The totally underdressed one? That's a definite no."

"You sure? He doesn't look like someone from the North Side? Or one of Rellik's guys?" I asked, trying not to sound desperate.

She shrugged. "Nope. Now let's go dance, Missy."

Maybe I was overreacting. Letting my nerves get the best of me.

Becca dragged me to the dance floor just as Juvenile came on. She knew exactly what that meant.

"Here we go, girl! Show me what that booty can do!" she yelled to the entire club.

I blushed, laughing, but decided to let go. For a minute, I forgot everything. The rules. The risks. Even Rellik.

I let the beat take over, and for the first time in a long time, I actually felt free.

I still scanned the room from time to time; old habits die hard. But 90% of the time, the coast looked clear.

The other 10%? VIP was still too dark to tell. And now the smoke machine had cranked up, adding another layer of haze. But it's not like Rellik's guys would be there, right?

I mean, this was the King's lair. It didn't even seem like any of the King's men were in here, though.

The buzz was starting to wear off, so I knew it was time for one more drink before calling it.

I headed to the bar. But before I picked a spot to stand, I glanced over my shoulder to check for him.

Gone.

"Vodka soda, please," I told the bartender.

She was small and mousy, quick with her hands, and while she mixed the drink, I took another long glance around the bar. By now, I should've been tipsy, maybe even laughing too loud with Becca. But I wasn't. I couldn't shake that guy's face from my head, that smile. Too wide. Too knowing.

The kind of smile that would make Ted Bundy proud.

And those eyes, they didn't just look at me. They locked on, like he was on a mission.

I swallowed hard. That eerie sensation of being watched crept up my spine again.

Shake it off, I told myself.

Just then, the bartender handed me my drink. I reached out to tell her to put it on Rebecca's tab, but…

"I got it," a voice said behind me.

I froze.

There he was again.

Same guy. Same creepy smirk. Now trying to pay for my drink.

"It's okay, we have a tab," I said, stumbling over my words.

He looked me up and down, slow and unbothered. That grin curled back across his face.

"No girl looking like you should ever have to pay for her drinks."

"I'm sorry, I'm not trying to be rude," I said carefully, "but do I know you?"

He stepped in closer. Way too close. I could feel the heat off him. He leaned in and whispered, his breath brushing my ear,

"Do you want to know me, North Sider?"

My stomach dropped. I stepped back immediately, eyes wide.

"H-how do you know I'm from the North Side? I mean, fuck."

"It's okay," he said casually, like we were sharing back and forth. "Your secret's safe with me. I just saw you and wanted to get to know you."

He was still closing the distance, inch by inch.

I planted my feet.

"Look, I don't know who you think I am, or how you know me, but I'm not interested. I'm just here to have a good time with my friend. So, thank you, but no thank you."

I backed away again, searching the dance floor for Becca. She was still dancing, completely oblivious, grinding on some guy like it was the last night on Earth.

Code. Fucking. Red.

But the bartender caught on. She gave me a glance, sharp and understanding, and I met her eyes in return. She nodded once and went into action.

"Hey, dude," she barked from across the bar, "back up. The lady said no, thank you."

He turned and shot her a glare, telling her to mind her own business, but the barback was already stepping up beside her.

"Okay, okay," he muttered, throwing up his hands.

"Just trying to make conversation. Maybe another time."

He walked off.

I exhaled.

"I have no idea how to thank you," I said, pulling a fifty from my wallet and dropping it into her tip jar. "Here, I know it's not enough, but seriously. Thank you."

"No thanks needed," she said, giving me a half-smile while her eyes looked behind me. "You can never be too careful. Us South Side ladies got to look out for each other, right?"

I nodded, but guilt twisted in my stomach.

I wasn't a South Side girl. I didn't belong here.

I put myself in this situation.

And I knew what I had to do next.

I made my way toward the dance floor to find Becca and tell her we were leaving. My gut was telling me to use rule number two and call Rellik immediately.

"Fuck, where is she?" I muttered, scanning the room in all directions. Panic started to bloom in my chest.

This was a bad idea. A fucking bad idea.

I never should've come to this side of town.

Rellik was going to kill me. I could already hear the lecture in my head.

I checked the bathroom, nothing. The bar is empty. She wasn't on the dance floor anymore, either. At this moment, I could not see Rebecca's red hair at all. That's how I usually found her, by her red hair and how tall she was.

By this point, I was ready to jump into the DJ booth and scream her name into the mic.

Where the hell could she be?

I looked up.

The VIP section.

Of course.

It was the only place I hadn't checked.

I started pushing through the crowd, making my way toward the roped-off stairs, when I felt a hand slide onto my hip.

Every instinct in my body fired off like a warning shot.

I spun around, ready to go into full defense mode.

"Excuse you, what the f..." I started, ready to swing.

But I froze.

It was him again.

I shoved him back. "Dude, take no for an answer. I'm not interested. Now leave me the hell alone."

My heart was racing. My mind scrambled. I couldn't even tell which direction the VIP section was anymore. I turned, trying to center myself. But before I could move, his hand clamped down on my wrist.

He pulled.

Instantly, I reacted. I twisted, wound up, ready to clock him, like Rellik had taught me.

But I didn't get the chance.

Before my fist could even head in his direction, there was a blur of motion beside me, a force, a tug, and then a thud.

The guy hit the ground.

Hard.

Even with the bass thumping and people yelling around me, I heard it. That unmistakable sound of a body slamming into the floor, like a stack of books crashing onto a school desk.

"OOOOOOOHHH!"

"Damn, bro! He's out cold!"

The crowd reacted before I did.

My eyes searched for Becca. Surely, she was the one who dropped him. That would be *so* her.

But she was nowhere in sight.

Instead, my gaze landed on someone else.

Someone I hadn't seen in years.

And the second I saw it, I knew.

The tattoo.

A crown.

As if it had always been a part of him, but it hadn't been. Not when I knew him. Not when I would lie beside him and count the freckles on his back or trace the veins in his arms.

Back then, his skin was clean.

Back then, he was mine.

But now.

Now he wore a crown.

The mark of a King.

The enemy.

And that meant I was completely and utterly fucked.

Suddenly, I was stone-cold sober.

I stopped breathing.

That wasn't just any crown tattoo.

The placement meant everything.

Not on his hand like the others. This was higher. Bolder. Intentional.

I knew what it meant because my brother made damn sure I knew everything about the Kings, the enemy.

I couldn't look away.

Every guy in The Kings had a crown tattoo. It was their mark. Their allegiance. But where they had it inked, it told you who they were.

Most guys wore it between the thumb and index finger.

But not this one.

Wrist tattoos were reserved for one person.

The Leader.

I swallowed hard, afraid to look up. But my mind was already spinning, galloping with questions like a runaway horse.

Had he been here all night?

Had he been watching me?

Was that why the bartender stepped in earlier?

Would he have let me leave without saying anything?

Or had he just shown up, right place, right time?

Was he in the VIP section the whole time, just out of view?

And more importantly.

Why?

Why did he intervene?

He stepped in like nothing had changed, like no time had passed.

Like the universe hadn't exploded the moment he disappeared from my life.

And just like that, I was back there.

Back before the crown tattoo.

Back before everything between him and my brother shattered.

Back before he vanished without a word.

The guy standing in front of me wasn't just some South Side stranger.

He was my brother's former best friend.

The boy who once held my heart.

And then broke it with his silence.

I hadn't seen him in years.

And now, here he was saving me without hesitation.

Still him.

Still the same eyes.

Still the same chaos behind them.

A thousand questions screamed through my head, racing faster than I could process.

But my body already knew.

I hadn't even looked up at his face.

But I didn't need to.

My pulse recognized him first, tightening in my throat, skipping in my chest.

The hairs on my arms rose.

Memories started coming in waves, crashing through my brain.

That voice.

That hand.

That pull.

And then I heard it.

Low. Dangerous. Familiar.

"Hello, Victoria," he whispered in my ear.

"Been a long time."

I bit my lower lip without realizing it.

Every inch of me is buzzing.

Every memory clawing its way to the surface.

It was him.

Vale. Fucking. Tino.

CHAPTER 2

Valentino.

The only person who calls me *Victoria*. No matter how many times I asked him to call me Tori, he refused. Always. I could never tell whether he did it to get under my skin or to show me he was in control. Making it seem that calling me Victoria was something special between us. Maybe it was both. Maybe being different was what he was trying to prove.

I took a slow, careful breath and looked up, trying not to blush as our eyes locked.

Those same dark brown eyes. The ones who used to study me as if I were the only thing in the world worth understanding. The ones that held me still without even touching me.

God, he hadn't changed. I slightly exhale, trying to grasp my thoughts together.

Valentino had the same tan skin that always caught the golden hour just right, and his jet-black hair was slicked back into a perfect ponytail bun. Almost seemed like it was his go-to, so that he was always ready. Always in control. Very different from the boy-next-door haircut that he had the last time I saw him.

I didn't move a muscle, but my eyes roamed. Traced. Took virtual screenshots, and then remembered.

He was tall, at least six feet two inches, with a lean, athletic build that didn't just wear clothes but owned them. Black slacks. Belted, pressed, tailored to his body like they were made just for him, and maybe they were. They clung to his hips in a way that made it impossible not to notice the way he moved, like every step had purpose, like the ground bent to meet him.

His long-sleeved black button-up hugged his torso, the fabric straining slightly over his chest and shoulders, enough to show the silhouette of his physique. The sleeves were rolled up to his forearms, exposing the kind of muscle that wasn't just for show, strong, defined, and laced with veins that pulsed subtly beneath his skin. The ones I used to trace lazily in the dark when I thought forever meant something.

He'd unbuttoned the top of his shirt, just low enough to give me a teasing glimpse of ink and skin, the start of a tattoo that stretched down across his chest, barely visible beneath the edge of the fabric. My gaze lingered there, caught on the ink, on the edge of his collarbone, on the memory of my mouth slowly kissing every inch of that area.

And then my eyes lifted past the sharp jawline, the clean shave, the mouth that had once kissed me like I was his only way of breathing. His cheekbones were more defined now, his features a little harder, but those eyes, dark, intense, watching me as if he could still see straight through me, hadn't changed.

Not one bit.

He was beautiful in the kind of way that made it hard to breathe. Not soft, not polished. Dangerous-beautiful. A walking warning label dressed in black, daring you to ignore it.

My stomach twisted, heat rushing to my cheeks before I could stop it. I hated that he looked like this. I hated that after everything, I still noticed, still wanted. Every piece of him felt like a dare, a temptation I had already lost to once and would lose to again if I wasn't careful. I quickly took one last glance.

And there it was, just as the one on his wrist.

The crown.

It wasn't there the last time I saw him; his neck had been bare.

But this wasn't fresh ink. This was new in the way everything about him had changed.

New since he decided to become **King**.

Since he decided to go after my brother, for reasons I still didn't understand.

It spanned the entire width of his throat, centered perfectly over his Adam's apple, like it was guarding something sacred. Five sharp points rose from the base, each crowned with a perfect, inked gemstone: deep violet, forest green, blood red, ocean blue, obsidian black. Amethyst, emerald, ruby, sapphire, and onyx.

Each one meant something: power, loyalty, protection, love, sacrifice.

I didn't need to ask what they meant, nor did I dare. The way he wore them told me everything. Like a declaration. Like a warning. Those crowns weren't for style; they were a statement of revenge, power, and maybe even war.

He didn't just mark his skin; he branded himself to send a message. A message for anyone who looked at THE CROWN. Deep down, I wondered, was that message initially made for Rellik, for me? Overall, I believe it was for anyone who remembered the boy who wholeheartedly cared for his ailing mother, walked the elderly across the street, and was just the regular boy next door. A message to show that the boy was gone.

Now he was something else entirely.

King.

The crown's base was etched in delicate, detailed linework, almost Druidic, like it belonged in an ancient spellbook or on a royal seal. And if you looked close enough, really close, you could see it.

Royalty.

The word was hidden inside the design, stretched like a whispered secret beneath the crown's roots. A name. A warning. A faint whisper.

It wasn't just a tattoo. It was armor.

A symbol of the boy who rose from nothing, who

bled for the crown he now carried. A boy who left everything and everyone he knew and loved. A boy who became a man, then a King, in a world built to crush him.

But even seeing and understanding everything the tattoo displayed wasn't what made me stop breathing. Literally.

It was the necklace.

An elegant, silver chain rested against his chest, the kind of metal that says weight, history, and durability. But hanging from the center, small and strange and devastatingly familiar, was a single pendant.

A Larkspur flower.

Its petals were soft purple, frozen between two circular panes of glass, preserved like something sacred, like something mourned.

And I knew it instantly.

That necklace was ours. Mine. Rellik's. His.

We gave it to him.

And somehow after all this time, after the silence, the betrayal, the abandonment, he still wore it.

I remember the day we picked it out, Rellik trying to act tough, pretending he didn't care, but I saw the way his jaw clenched every time Vale's name came up. He was hurting too. We both were. Papi had just died weeks prior; I was still in shambles, and Rellik kept me close due to dangers still out there. Even

Vale was acting differently those weeks, more distant, protective, and conflicted. Now it was his turn to be in shambles. Vale's mother had just died, and he'd shut down, pulled back from everyone, even Rellik. I was the one who found the flower first. *Larkspur*. July's flower. She was born in July, and it was the same month that we lost them both.

When I showed it to Rellik, he didn't say a word. Just took the pendant, paid for it without hesitation, and muttered something like, "Vale needs something to hold onto."

When we gave it to him, Vale didn't cry. He didn't speak. He just stared at it for a long moment, then slipped the chain over his neck and tucked the pendant under his shirt like he was hiding a piece of his heart.

And now, years later, it was still there hanging from his neck, right above his chest, right over the place where he buried every damn feeling he refused to show.

It wasn't just jewelry. It was proof.

Proof that once, we meant something to him. Rellik and I. That we mattered. That even when everything else went to hell, when secrets were buried, and hearts were broken, we had been real. I had been real.

And now, standing here, staring at that pendant again, I couldn't help but wonder.

If he still wore that piece, had he ever truly moved on? Why build this entire Kingdom and still have something so sacred from someone whom you are supposed to hate, and from someone who you ghosted so many years ago?

Suddenly, the club felt hotter, like the A/C had shut off hours ago. I was practically melting where I stood. Hoping my setting spray was working. My heart was pounding, trying to block out the memories that were clawing their way back in.

But I knew the truth.

Once he smiled, I would fold like the piece of cheese I had on my omelet this morning.

I always fell for his smile. I could never stay mad at him, not when those damn dimples showed.

By now, the memories had officially broken the wall that I had placed to protect myself. Not just memories, details.

Vale and I didn't just have history. At one point, he was considered family.

He was Rellik's best friend since they were kids. And he was the first man in my bed.

"Vale," I said sternly, forcing the name out like it didn't still taste like longing. I prayed he wouldn't notice how badly my body wanted to inch closer.

"Victoria, why are you here?" he asked, voice low and eyes hard. Disapproval lined every syllable.

Seriously? That's what he had to say to me?

The last time I saw Valentino was in my bedroom.

Making all these promises.

And now he's interrogating me like I'm the problem?

Anger, embarrassment, guilt, they hit all at once.

I remember how it started. Valentino was always at our house. He and Rellik were inseparable.

Back then, I thought it was harmless. Two boys being boys, loud, obnoxious, constantly testing boundaries. But there were moments, these tiny moments, when I'd catch Vale watching me from the corner of his eye, like he wasn't supposed to, but couldn't help himself.

At first, I thought I was imagining it. Maybe my schoolgirl crush was getting the best of me.

Then came the nights.

There were nights when he stayed later than usual. Nights when I'd hear them laughing downstairs and then silence. A knock on my bedroom door.

It always started the same.

"You up?"

I wasn't supposed to be part of their world. I was Rellik's little sister. Off-limits. Untouchable.

But one night, everything blurred.

He kissed me like he was drowning and I was the only air left.

And I let him.

Again and again.

Until the night, everything shattered.

"You don't get to ask me why I'm here," I said, quieter than I meant to, but firmer than he deserved. "Not after disappearing like you did."

His expression flickered, just for a second. But it was enough.

"I'm taking you home. Now," he snarled.

"No," I hissed, stepping back like his presence was something I could dodge. "You don't get to boss me around; you have no authority over me."

"Victoria," he growled, "I am taking you the fuck home. Now, you can either walk to my car, or I can carry your ass. Your choice."

I stared in awe at him. Did he just say that?

There's no way in hell he'd carry me out of this club.

So, I decided to call his bluff.

(Okay, maybe not the right choice.)

"You don't control me. I'm not your girlfriend, and I sure as hell am not your property." My voice was shaking, but I didn't back down. "I'm tired of being controlled. Now, back off and let me have some fun."

He took a deep breath, lifting his left eyebrow.

At that moment, I literally just wanted him to take me, take me anywhere. But no. I stood my ground. I kept reminding myself that I was angry and hurt.

Valentino looked around once, slowly, and then turned back to me.

And without warning, he threw me over his shoulder and started walking out.

I screamed, pounding on his back, "*¡Suéltame*, put me down!"

He snarled, low and possessive, "Not my property, huh? You're mine. You've always been mine, whether you knew it or not. Why do you think they ghosted you? I made them leave. Because you will always be my Queen. Now shut up and let me take you home."

He stormed toward the exit with me still slung over his shoulder like I weighed nothing. I was pounding on his back, shouting for him to put me down, and everyone in the club had stopped to stare, some with even cameras out.

Then someone stepped in his way.

"Yo, what the hell do you think you're—"

The guy didn't finish his sentence.

Vale turned his head just slightly, his jaw ticking, one look.

That was all it took.

The guy's face went pale, like he'd seen a ghost or worse. "Shit," he muttered, stumbling back. "Didn't know it was you, Sir. My bad. Real bad."

He pulled his friend with him as if proximity alone might get him hurt. No one else dared speak.

That's the thing about Valentino Costa.

He doesn't have to raise his voice. He doesn't even have to say a word.

He *is* the threat.

My mind blanked, then replayed what he just said in my head all over again.

Did he say what I think he said?

All this time, is that why nobody ever asked me out? Why they bailed? Was Valentino pulling strings behind the scenes like Rellik does with everything else in my life?

What in the actual fuck.

I was furious. I was stunned. But mostly, I was so turned on, I didn't know how to breathe.

He gently placed me in the passenger seat of his car, then walked around the front and slid into the driver's side. He threw his jacket, which was handed to him at the door, in the back seat. As he sat there, the light hit just right, revealing the whole sleeve of tattoos that I imagined were on there. That's when I caught it, a glimpse of the number 14 inked just above his elbow.

I stared.

It can't be.

It must be a coincidence. Or maybe it meant something else. It had to.

But he caught my expression, and without even looking at me, said, "You think I'd forget that day? That's the day you promised you were mine."

I was speechless.

The memory hit me like a freight train.

All those years ago, I still remembered every moment, every spark, every slow, dangerous shift in the air between us. It started when Rellik's practice ran late. I was at home, working on a project in my room, when Vale walked in. I told him my brother wasn't home, and he responded that he came to see me, not Rellik.

He sat on the edge of my bed like he belonged there, watching me underline a sentence in my notebook like it was the most captivating thing in the world. I felt his eyes on me like a spotlight I hadn't asked for, but didn't want turned off.

"You know," he said, voice casual, "you've got this little line right here."

He reached out and traced just beneath my chin with his finger. "It shows up when you're focused. It's cute."

I looked up at him, narrowing my eyes. "That's a weird thing to say."

"Not if you've been noticing it for a while."

That was his first move.

Subtle.

Smooth.

No warning.

I laughed it off, but inside, I was on fire. And from that day on, something changed.

He started hanging around even when Rellik wasn't there, when my dad was working late. Staying later. Watching me longer. Dropping small comments that only I was meant to hear.

Like the time he murmured, "If you weren't Rellik's sister..."

And didn't finish the sentence.

Or when he leaned behind me in the kitchen, whispering, "You look gorgeous today," before walking away like it meant nothing.

At first, it was flirtation. Stolen glances. Lingering touches. Moments that didn't quite cross a line, but danced dangerously close.

He pushed my buttons. I never pushed back.

We didn't plan for it to go that far, but it always felt inevitable. It felt like we were destined from the beginning to be with each other. We just needed the one little push.

The first time it happened, it was storming.

Rellik had left to meet someone. Said he wouldn't be back for hours. Dad was out on business. I was on the couch watching TV, trying to pretend everything was normal. Trying not to let Vale's eyes on me twist me up inside.

Then the power went out. The whole house went black.

I jumped.

He laughed, low, deep, and familiar. That laugh always undid me.

"You scared of the dark, Victoria?" he teased.

I didn't answer.

He crossed the room and sat beside me. Our knees touched. My breath caught.

And then he kissed me.

It wasn't gentle, not at first. It was years of built-up tension crashing all at once like waves hitting the docks. He pulled me into his lap and kissed me like I was the last thing holding him together.

That night, I gave him every piece of me.

It wasn't just sex. It was more than that. It was a promise neither of us said out loud. A secret buried between the sheets, under the weight of everything we knew we'd lose if we got caught.

And we did get caught, not by Rellik, or even my father, but by time.

Because the last time I saw Vale was just a month later.

Weeks had passed. Papi's death had taken a toll on all of us. Vale's mother lost her battle to cancer as well. We were young and hurting. But one thing I had was Vale; he was my anchor, my lifeline. We were in my room again. He kissed my shoulder like he always did and whispered that he was going to tell Rellik the truth. Said he couldn't keep pretending. These past few weeks, he knew he was distant, but that my love for him was all that he needed to survive.

"I want this out in the open," he said. "I want us to be real."

I told him that no matter what Rellik said, I was his. Always. Forever. And that was the night we decided. We marked the fourteenth as our day. The one that would start our lives together. Our clean start. Our quiet rebellion turned loud. He even made me promise, "No backing out. No hiding."

I was nervous, sure. Terrified, even. But more than anything, I was ready. Ready to finally stop pretending, prepared to face the fallout if it meant being his.

But the fourteenth didn't come the way I imagined.

I waited for him all night.

No call. No knock on the door. Just silence.

He was gone.

No explanation. No warning. Like everything we said, everything we felt, had been swallowed up by the dark.

Days turned into weeks.

Rellik never mentioned him again. No slip, no hint, not even a passing curse. It was like Vale had never existed at all, like I'd imagined him, dreamt him into existence.

And I started to believe maybe I had.

How do you explain someone who vanishes without a trace?

How do you mourn someone who was never officially lost?

I lost Papi and then Vale.

All within the same month.

Two men who meant everything to me, gone, like they were never mine to keep.

And while I was drowning in grief, something strange began to happen.

Whispers started to circle the South Side.

A new crew was rising. Ruthless. Sharp. Untouchable.

They called themselves **The Kings.**

No one knew who led them, at first.

But I recognized the rumors. The style. The quiet precision.

And then Rebecca told me what she heard.

That there was a man.

A man who knew all of Rellik's moves.

A man who was out to destroy **The Killers**, one by one.

She said his people call him **King Vale**.

Said they tattooed crowns on their skin as a sign of loyalty.

Said he ruled from the shadows, unbothered and untouchable.

He'd vanished from my life.

And in the ashes of whatever we were.

He built an empire.

He didn't just disappear.

He reinvented himself.

And I broke. Quietly. Slowly.

I went on with my life because I had to. Smiled when I was supposed to, played the good little sister Rellik needed. But inside, I was hollow. Cracked glass barely holding shape. And no one, not even my brother, ever knew how close I came to shattering.

Now he's sitting beside me again.

Valentino.

Alive. Breathing.

Staring straight ahead as if none of it had happened.

And all I can think is…

Why did you leave me?

I didn't say it out loud. But God, I wanted to. My throat burned from holding it in, like it had been sitting there for years, waiting to break free.

The silence in the car was thick, matching the heavy tension. Unforgiving.

Vale gripped the steering wheel tightly. His jaw flexed once, twice. I could feel him battling something, words he wanted to say but wouldn't let escape. Still, he didn't look at me.

Coward.

"You disappeared," I finally murmured, the words trembling even though I tried to sound strong. "No goodbye. No explanation. Just gone."

He glanced at me. Barely. Just long enough for me to see the storm behind his eyes, and for him to see the redness begin around mine.

"I had my reasons."

"You always do, don't you?"

The car filled with silence again, but this time it wasn't heavy; it was jagged. Sharp with everything unsaid.

My heart was still racing, partly from the fight and partly from being this close to him. But something else crept in, too, uncertainty.

I turned slightly. "That guy in the bar. The one who grabbed me. What did you do to him?"

Vale didn't answer for a long moment. Just stared straight ahead like he was trying to decide how much to give me.

"He'll live," he said finally. "But he won't touch anyone like that again."

"Jesus," I muttered.

"I warned them." His voice was calm. Too calm. "No one puts hands on my Queen."

I didn't respond. Because part of me wanted to be furious, and the other part? The other part was sickly, dangerously turned on.

I let out a dry laugh and looked out the window. The city lights blurred with the heat rising behind my eyes.

And then it hit me.

"Shit, Rebecca." I sat up straighter, eyes darting back toward the city disappearing behind us. "She was still inside when you pulled me out. I didn't even…"

"She's safe," Vale said, his voice even. "One of my guys is walking her out the back now. I made sure."

"You, what?" I turned to look at him, blinking. "How do you even remember who she is?"

His grip on the steering wheel tightened just slightly.

"I never really left you. I've been watching from a distance."

I swallowed hard. "She's going to be worried. She's probably already calling Rellik."

He gave a slight shake of his head. "She isn't. She told my guy she will not give Rellik a reason to start a war unless she has the full story. Said to tell you to text her when you're safe."

That made something twist in my stomach, guilt mainly. For leaving her. For getting caught up in something that still had claws in me.

"She didn't even try to stop you?" I whispered.

"She saw the look on your face," he said, glancing at me. "She didn't have to."

Vale exhaled, long and low, like he'd been holding his breath for years. "You think I liked doing this? Walking away from you?" His voice was hoarse. "Every day since, I've lived like I'm missing a limb."

I turned my head toward him again, jaw clenched. "Then why didn't you reach out? A call, a letter, anything."

He tapped the steering wheel with each finger, starting from the pinky to the index, agitated. "Because I didn't deserve to."

"Don't you dare put that on me," I snapped. "You don't get to decide what I deserve. You disappeared and left me in pieces when I was at my most vulnerable."

His voice dropped to a whisper, but it still cut like a blade. "I was trying to keep you safe."

"From what?" I demanded. "Say it, Vale. Stop hiding behind half-truths and noble bullshit. You think I needed protecting? I needed you."

He looked at me then, thoroughly. His eyes weren't just dark, they were wrecked. Torn. "You don't know what I was involved in. What I had to do."

"Then tell me," I said, quieter now. "Give me something to hold on to, or let me go for good."

The words hung in the air, heavy with everything we'd never said. But Vale just gripped the wheel tighter, his silence saying more than any confession ever could.

His knuckles whitened. "You think this was easy for me?"

I turned to him, entirely. "You think I care? I gave you everything, Valentino. You crawled into my bed, into my life, and then you vanished like I was just a fucking phase. So, no, I don't care if it was easy for you."

He slammed the brakes at a red light, both of us jolting forward slightly from the force. He turned to me sharply, eyes burning.

"You were never a fucking phase."

The words were low, guttural. Real.

My chest rose and fell faster. I swallowed hard, not trusting myself to say one word.

The light turned green, but he didn't move.

"I had to protect you," he said finally. "You don't understand the shit that was happening. I was deeper than anyone knew. And if I stayed, that would have been the end, the end of everything."

"Bullshit," I whispered. "You left, and it was the end."

He didn't deny it. Just stared through the windshield, jaw ticking.

And then, softer, almost like he was speaking to himself, he muttered.

"I made a decision that night, one that I'll pay for the rest of my life."

I froze. My breath caught.

That night.

That same night, he said he would tell Rellik the truth.

The same night, he never came back.

"What happened, Vale?"

He shook his head once, like he was trying to erase something. "Not tonight."

I wanted to scream. Grab his face and force him to look at me. To feel everything I was still feeling. But I didn't. I sat there, arms crossed tight over my chest, and said nothing else the whole ride home.

When he pulled up in front of my apartment, he killed the engine but didn't move.

"I didn't forget about you, Victoria," he said quietly. "There hasn't been a single night I haven't thought about you. Or regretted my decisions that led up to everything."

I didn't answer. Couldn't. Because I wasn't sure if I wanted to kiss him or slap him.

He finally turned to me, voice rough.

"Go inside before I do something stupid."

I opened the door and stepped out.

But just before I shut it, I said without looking back.

"You already did."

CHAPTER 3

I didn't turn around. Even though every part of me wanted to. I kept telling myself, keep walking, you're almost at the door. Do not turn around. Not even once.

I could feel him watching me as I walked to the front door. The weight of his stare burned a hole right through me, as if I were outside on a hot summer day with a magnifying glass staring at the sun. My keys rattled in my hand. I was shaking and trying my hardest to pretend I wasn't. I hated that he still had that effect on me. This control over me. Hated even more that I didn't want it to stop.

I pushed the door open and stepped inside, letting it close behind me with a soft click. My apartment was dark except for the glow of the streetlights bleeding through the blinds. I didn't flip a switch. I just stood there, breath shallow, back pressed to the door like I was bracing for something.

The faint sound of my bedroom fan humming was distant in the silence. My heartbeat echoed louder than anything else. I started rummaging through my purse for my phone to turn it on and message Rebecca. My anxiety starts to kick in like clockwork. I pressed my hand to my chest like that might calm it.

It didn't.

And then I heard it. Over the humming, my heartbeat, and the startup noise from my phone. His car door.

Followed by his footsteps.

He didn't even hesitate.

A second later, there was a knock. Not loud. Not demanding. Just there. A simple rhythm, like a question. *Can I come in?*

I stared at my faded winter blue door, knowing damn well who was standing there behind it. I knew that if I opened it, I wouldn't be able to keep my stance much longer. Not that I hated him. Not that I'd moved on. Not that I didn't still ache for every touch, every lie, every truth we never got to speak. It's just too much, all in one night.

I didn't answer.

I could hear his feet rambling from behind the door. A shift even.

I opened the door.

I stood by the frame, hand still clinging to the knob like it might anchor me to a decision I hadn't made yet. The tension between us was substantial, with everything we hadn't said. My heart was pounding so hard, I was sure he could hear it.

Valentino stepped toward me, slow, careful, like I was something fragile he didn't want to scare away. His voice dropped, and you could see the expression on his face as he prepared for what he was about to say.

"I have been a liar and a cheat," he said, eyes locked on mine. "I know that I've caused you heartache and pain."

My throat tightened, my body tensed up. I didn't say a word. I couldn't. I just listened. Having no clue what he was going to say next, or how I was going to respond.

"But I will drop to my knees and give you the keys to my kingdom," he whispered, voice trembling now, "to have one more night with you."

He paused long enough for the weight of his words to settle in the air between us.

"If that's what it takes to be near you." He said softly, "I'll burn it all down. Walk away from every throne, every crown, every soldier in my name. Just say the word."

He was close enough now that I could feel his heat and his breath all at once. Close enough that if I leaned forward just a few inches, I'd be in his arms again.

And my body remembered him before my mind permitted it, the way he used to pull me in like he was starving. The warmth of his breath against my collarbone when he whispered promises he'd never keep.

I blinked, trying to steady myself, to hold back the flood that was pushing to come through. I let out a tear, as much as I was trying not to show any emotion. But every piece of me was screaming. Every part that had once belonged to him still did. And that terrified me more than anything.

I shook my head just slightly, as the words slipped out, delicate but heavy with meaning.

"When did it become breaking a rule to say your name out loud?"

He didn't respond; he couldn't. His eyes dropped for the first time, and in that small silence, something cracked inside me.

"I was suffering when you left just like that," I said, my voice sharper now, trembling but firm. "I felt like I was nothing to you. Just some girl you needed to fulfill your needs. Disposable."

His head snapped back, pain flashing across his face. But I didn't stop.

"You disappeared, Vale. No explanation. No goodbye. You broke me when I was already broken. And then it was as if you never existed."

My voice cracked, but I kept going. "My dad had just died. I was already falling apart, and you knew that. And I know you were hurting too after your mom died. You held me the night we buried him, and I held you when it was your mom. You said we didn't have to go through it alone." My throat tightened. "But then you left. And suddenly, I was grieving two ghosts."

I saw it hit him, harder than I think he expected. But that didn't stop me. I had years to practice this in my head, and it was all coming out.

"And I tried to make excuses for you. Told myself maybe it was too much for you, too. Maybe it was about your mom, and you couldn't say it out loud. But that didn't make it hurt less. That didn't stop me from waking up every night thinking maybe you'd call. Maybe you'd show up."

I swallowed, fighting to stay steady. "But you didn't. And I had to pretend like none of it mattered, like I hadn't just lost everything in the same breath."

He didn't move. Didn't blink. Just stood there, like he was absorbing every word like a blade to the chest. His eyes showed defeat, desperation, and anguish. Then, finally, he spoke, soft but trembling with conviction.

"For years, in all my dreams, you were lost and never found," he said. "The thought of you not by my side was ripping me apart. I made a promise."

His voice caught, like there was more he wanted to say but couldn't. He exhaled sharply and looked at me again, eyes burning like wildfire.

"But the moment you walked into my club, everything went out the window, promises, loyalty, everything. Nothing that I had said or done mattered anymore."

I hesitated. "Promises?" I echoed, the word tasting like pennies on my tongue. "Loyalty to whom, Vale? What the hell does that even mean?"

His jaw tightened. Just slightly. A muscle tensed in

his cheek, but he didn't answer.

"Was it about Rellik?" I asked, sharper now. "Was it about the Kings? Was it about me?"

Still, nothing.

"Say it," I demanded, my voice cracking. "Say what pulled you away from me that night. Pulled you away from having everything out in the open, like we wanted. Say, what was worth throwing everything away for?"

His eyes flicked up to mine for the briefest second and then away. "It's not that simple."

"It never is with you," I whispered bitterly. "You say words like promises and loyalty like they mean something, but you won't let me in. You left me with nothing, emotionally severed, and now you expect me to pretend that doesn't matter?"

His breath caught, but he still didn't speak. And that silence that refusal was louder than anything he could've said.

He looked at me, really looked at me, and the air between us shifted. Thickened, solidified into something that could almost be seen.

His gaze wasn't just on me; it was inside me. Tearing through every wall I'd built. Finding the girl who used to wait for him in the dark, the one who never stopped waiting.

My throat ached with all the things I couldn't say. My fists clenched at my sides, knuckles pale. By this time, my purse was already on the floor, and all I wanted to do was scream. I wanted to cry. I wanted to touch him and hit him in the very same breath.

He stepped a little closer. Barely. Testing the waters to see what I would allow.

"I thought about you every single day," he said, voice low. "I know I don't deserve to say that. But I did, I do. Every day, Victoria."

His voice was raw when he said my name, like it still meant something sacred to him. Like it still had a pulse.

I looked up at him, my eyes devoured in tears, and something inside me shattered all over again. He wasn't just standing there; he was pleading without words, pleading with the silence. With the pain carved into every line of his face. With the way his hand trembled at his side, like he wanted to reach for me, but didn't know if he had the right. The man who stood there looking right at me was not *King Vale* but the Vale I knew and felt in my heart and body.

And the worst part?

I wanted him.

So damn badly.

I didn't move. I didn't give him permission.

I didn't have to.

Because he took that one final step.

And I fell.

He grabbed me by the waist and pulled me to him in one fluid motion, like his body had been craving mine for years. His mouth crashed against mine with desperation, nothing soft, nothing sweet. It was all tongue and heat and breathless hunger. My hands went to his shirt, yanking it open the rest of the way, buttons scattering like they'd been waiting for this moment as long as I had. I needed to feel him. Skin to skin. Proof that he was real. This was real, and not all in my head.

But I broke the kiss, just for a second. Just long enough to breathe. Just long enough to say the one thing I'd never said out loud.

"You left when I was at my weakest," I whispered, my forehead pressed against his, my breath catching. "My home was no longer a home, Rellik and I were drowning, and I couldn't sleep. I couldn't eat. And you knew that. You knew how shattered I was."

His eyes searched mine, wide with something like sorrow, but I didn't stop.

"Your mom was sick, and then she was gone. And I was trying to be there for you, even when I was barely holding it together myself. I was scared, Vale. I felt like I was losing everything and everyone. And then you vanished like none of it mattered. No explanation. No goodbye. Just gone."

My voice cracked. "I had nightmares, I would wake up screaming,"

He closed his eyes, jaw tight, the pain etched deeper now. He looked like he wanted to say something, but couldn't.

"I thought maybe you died, too," I admitted, barely a whisper now. "That's how bad it got. I checked the obituaries every day. I walked past alleyways and wondered if you were lying in one of them. And when I stopped looking."

My voice broke completely. "I hated myself for it."

My lips trembled. "I needed you. I needed someone. And the only person I ever trusted other than my brother or Rebecca just disappeared."

Another tear slipped out before I could stop it. His thumb brushed it away, gently but aching.

"It's not like I wanted to disappear," he murmured. "If I could go back—"

"You can't," I cut in. Not harsh. Just honest. "We can't go back."

Another beat of silence. The air between us buzzed with the weight of everything we'd just unburied.

And still, despite it all, despite the pain, the wreckage, the pieces of myself he'd once left behind, I still wanted him.

I still ached for him in a way that defied reason.

Because he wasn't just the boy who left me.

He was the boy I loved before I knew what love could cost.

He moved again, slower this time. His hands cradled my face like I was something precious. And when his lips met mine again, it wasn't desperate this time.

I shouldn't have wanted this. I should've screamed at him, pushed him away, demanded more answers, but instead, I pulled him closer.

"Fuck," he groaned into my mouth. "You drive me crazy."

"Then leave," I panted, tugging him toward the bedroom.

"Can't."

He said it like a vow, like he couldn't stay away even if it killed him.

I stared at him, my pulse in my throat, every nerve ending screaming at me to slam the door shut. To protect what was left of me.

But I didn't.

Because some part of me, the reckless, aching part, was still his.

The door barely shut behind us before he pushed me against it, hands everywhere, my neck, my hips, under my shirt. He didn't undress me like I was breakable. He stripped me like he owned me, and I let him, because part of me still did.

My back hit the mattress, and he followed, kissing down my chest, tracing the curve of my breast with his tongue like he was memorizing it all over again. My breath hitched when his hand slid between my thighs, fingers moving slowly, calculated, coaxing moans I hadn't let out in years.

"Vale," I whispered.

He looked up, eyes burning. "Say it again."

His lips hovered above mine, his breath hot. "Say it again."

I looked at him, really looked, and it was like seeing the boy he used to be light up beneath the man he'd become.

I swallowed. "Vale."

He groaned and kissed me like my name on his lips was a drug. Every movement was filled with the kind of intensity that only comes from years of silence. It wasn't just lust. It was pain. Regret. Love, we weren't allowed to say out loud.

When he finally entered me, I gasped, clawing at his back, because it wasn't just my body that remembered him; it was my soul. His motion was slow at first, like he wanted to make it last. But when I wrapped my legs around him and pulled him in deeper, everything snapped.

"Goddamn, I missed you," he spoke softly against my neck, his rhythm quickening. "You feel like home."

Tears slipped from the corners of my eyes, but I didn't stop him. I didn't stop myself. Because in that moment, I needed to believe it. Needed to believe we were more than whatever wreckage we'd left behind.

I clung to him like he was the last oxygen I was allowed before my last breath.

Maybe this wasn't forgiveness or closure.

Maybe it was just survival.

We came together with strangled bodies shaking, limbs tangled in heat and sweat, and everything unsaid. And for a second, it was as if only we existed in this cruel world.

When the room finally stilled, Vale lay beside me, his arm draped across my waist, his face buried in my neck. We didn't talk at first.

"I didn't just leave because I wanted to." He paused.

I turned my face toward him but stayed quiet. My heart was pounding. I didn't trust myself to speak.

"Things were going on," he continued, "shit, I never wanted you near. My mom was sick, and it got bad. Bills piled up. Treatments weren't working. I was desperate."

He swallowed hard. "I made a choice. One I'll regret for the rest of my life."

I studied his profile in the low light, the tightness in his jaw, the rawness just beneath it. God, I wanted to believe him. Wanted to fall into his arms and pretend like the world hadn't ripped us apart. But the scars were still there. Still fresh as if it were yesterday.

"You should've told me," I whispered. "I would've helped."

He turned to me then. Finally, his eyes were dark, vulnerable in a way I'd never seen before.

"I couldn't let you help, Victoria. I needed to fix it. I needed to be…" He paused, voice trembling. "Tell me you don't believe that we all fall down sometimes."

The way he said it, like he wasn't asking for forgiveness, just understanding, tore through me. It wasn't just a question. It was a confession, a plea.

I reached out, tracing the edge of his tattoo absently, feeling the beat of his heart through my fingertips.

"I do," I said, my voice cracking. "But you didn't just fall, Vale. You disappeared."

His eyes shut like my words physically hurt him.

And suddenly, I was back there, those last few days, when everything started to feel off.

He'd grown distant. Guilty. Constantly checking his phone, trying his best to be there for me as I grieve. But handling things so differently. Even his relationship with Rellik had seemed to change.

I remembered lying in bed with him one night, his body tense even as he held me. I traced the line of his jaw, trying to memorize him in the dark.

"You're not really here, are you?" I whispered.

He didn't answer. Just kissed my forehead and pulled me closer. But even then, I felt it, like he was already halfway gone.

Another night, I followed him, just once. Not for too

long. But once he headed to Dead Mile, the stretch of railroad tracks that marks the land between territories, I turned back. Rellik always warned me not to go there because it was too dangerous.

I didn't confront him. I couldn't. But I remembered sitting on the edge of my bed, staring at the spot where his hoodie still hung on my doorknob, and thinking, what the hell was he getting into?

I shoved away the memory. The ache in my chest was old but sharp, like it had only been waiting to be reawakened.

I lay back down, inching away just slightly, needing space but not wanting him to leave.

"Stay," I said quietly.

"I wasn't going anywhere," Vale answered.

I didn't say anything. I was too emotional to. I just shifted closer, burying myself into his chest, like maybe I could push the past into nonexistence.

But deep down, the question still burned.

What did you do, Vale?

And would knowing the answer finally kill what was left of me?

Or was the truth the only way to survive it?

I must've drifted to sleep like that, my cheek against his chest, our bodies still tangled under the weight of everything we couldn't say.

But it didn't last long, maybe an hour or so. No sunrise, not just yet. Just a sharp buzz vibrating on the floor where my phone had landed sometime during our whole conversation.

My eyes were still heavy as I stirred, but the moment I saw the screen lighting up, my blood ran cold.

17 missed calls.

9 voicemails.

14 unread texts.

All from one name: **Rellik.**

There was one call and one text from John before the hurricane of Rellik.

I sat up too fast, the sheet slipping from my shoulders. My fingers shook as I reached for the phone, unlocking it with a swipe that nearly missed.

The first message hit me like a punch to the chest.

Rellik: *Where the fuck are you?*

Then.

Rellik:

Tori. Call me back.

Ahora Mismo.

This isn't a joke.

I swear to God...

Why am I getting reports that you went to the South Side?

Did you go looking for him?

You deliberately broke our rules!

What the fuck! He carried you out?

Literally, I am watching the video now!

TORI, You FUCKING better not be with him!!!!!

Answer the phone, NOW!

¿Me entiendes?

The room tilted. My lungs forgot how to work. Each new notification lit up the screen like a fuse, and the panic exploded before I could stop it.

I couldn't breathe.

I couldn't think.

All I could hear was my brother's voice in my head, razor-sharp.

TORI, You FUCKING better not be with him.

He's going to kill him.

He's going to kill me.

"I, I can't." I gasped, clutching at my chest. "I can't breathe."

"Victoria?" Vale's voice was low and rough with sleep, but the second he saw me, he snapped fully awake. He sat up fast, eyes wide. "Hey, hey, look at me."

But I couldn't. I was already falling apart, spiraling past fear, past reason, past anything I could hold onto.

He was in front of me in seconds, kneeling on the floor between my legs, gripping my shoulders gently, firmly.

"Victoria. *Mírame*. Right here," he said, voice low and solid, like an anchor.

I forced myself to look at him through the blur of tears.

"You're okay," he said. "Just breathe with me, alright? In..."

He inhaled slowly, showing me.

"...and out."

I tried. God, I tried.

"Again. In. Out."

The air still caught in my throat, trying to push through it, my focus narrowed to nothing but the sound of his voice and the rise of his chest. He was slowly becoming my anchor.

"You're safe. I promise, you're safe. No one's going to hurt you. I've got you."

His hands moved up to my face, brushing the hair off my cheeks, wiping tears I didn't even realize were still falling.

"That's it," he whispered, his forehead resting against mine. "That's my girl. I've got you."

Little by little, the pressure started to lift. My breathing slowed. My heart still raced, but I wasn't drowning anymore. Shaking yes, but not drowning. Technically, I think I was rocking back and forth.

I collapsed into him, letting his arms wrap around me again.

"I'm sorry," I whispered, my voice cracking. "I didn't know, I didn't think he..."

"Shh. It's not your fault."

"But he knows," I said, pulling back just enough to see his face. "Vale, he knows I am with you. He's going to come for you."

"I don't care," he said, holding me tighter. "Let him come."

I shook my head, panic rising again. "Don't say that."

"I'm not afraid of Rellik," he said quietly. "I'm only afraid of losing you again."

That disrupted something inside me. Not in a painful way. Just in a way that made me stop running for a second. Made me want to believe that maybe, just maybe, we could survive this.

I wiped my face with the back of my hand and took another breath, this one a little stronger than the last.

"We have to be careful," I whispered.

He nodded. "We will be."

But in the pit of my stomach, I already knew the truth.

It was too late.

CHAPTER 4

The sun peeked through the blinds, just hitting my face enough to rise. When I fully woke, I gently moved my arm next to me to feel his touch once again. But it was empty, warm, but empty.

 I cautiously sat up, the sheet slipping down my bare chest as I listened. No footsteps, no water from a shower or sink. Just silence.

I slipped out of bed, looking around at first. I started moving silently toward the door and opened it just enough to peek.

He was there.

A quilt of relief overcame me. He stayed.

Vale stood out by the window in deep thought, shirt draped over one shoulder, staring out at the street as if he was waiting for a sign or perhaps an army. The early light hit him at angles. Sharp jaw, tense shoulders, every ridge of muscle that it could touch. His dark hair was no longer unruly from everything that had happened between us; you could tell he took the time to fix it and look like a King once again. It was slicked back in a topknot twist, like he hadn't thought twice about it.

I let my eyes roam down his back, past the structure of his arms and the way his tattoos curved over muscles like they belonged there, like they were a part of him, branded in flesh and ink. The waistband of his pressed pants hung low on his hips, just slightly exposing the V. I felt heat rise in areas of my body, once again entirely on the memory of how effortlessly he had unraveled me just hours ago, and how I allowed it.

All this time that I was watching, he hadn't noticed, at least not yet. I continued to watch just a little longer, watching the man who once shattered me and yet still made me blush by just giving me one small glance.

"Why do you always leave before I wake up?" I asked, my voice softer than I meant it to be.

He turned, slightly stunned, like he hadn't realized I was there. Our eyes met, and I saw that gleam of guilt, of longing, of something raw he hadn't shown in years. What exactly was going through his head? Regret, perhaps?

"I didn't want to," he said, voice rough. "But I didn't know how long to stay."

I crossed my arms, still holding the sheet tight around me, making sure the neighbors didn't get a free show. "Then leave." I scoffed.

He took a step forward, just one, enough to close the space and view of me to the street, but not enough to touch. I could smell him, sandalwood and something primal, with a hint of darkness underneath it all.

"I want to stay. You must know that. However, there are still things I haven't told you. The last thing I want is to give you any more pain than I have already caused you."

Air stalled in my lungs, just briefly. Part of me wanted to reach for him, to touch every muscle on his chest with my fingertips and wrap him around my sheet. The other part remembered the hollowness I felt after he left, not hearing from him for so long. Playing back our last night together over and over and questioning everything. Never knowing what I may have done wrong to deserve that.

Vale took a step back, finally breaking our gaze, and slipped his arms into the sleeves of his shirt. He started to fasten the buttons, or at least what was left of them. I watched as the muscles along his stomach tensed. I tried to look away, but I was locked in. I didn't know if I was going to see him again. And in that moment, he looked younger, less like the man that everyone seemed to know, and more like the boy I once loved. I blushed.

Just before he walked away, he paused, keys in hand.

"I meant what I said last night, Victoria. About loving you. That never changed."

And then he walked away.

All that was left behind was the ghost of his touch and the weight of all the things that were said.

I walk back in, hearing the door click behind me. As I leaned against it, I noticed that Vale waited to drive away until I was back inside. The atmosphere was different, emptier, but still electrifying. I try to catch my breath, my thoughts, and, overall, think about what my next step will be. I sat back in my recliner, the sheet still tightly wrapped around me, my skin reminiscing about every touch.

What the hell am I doing?

As I got dressed, my thoughts started to unravel. Why did I allow all of this to happen? Letting him in. Letting him touch me. Letting myself feel again. Every part of me screamed it was a mistake. But my body didn't care. My heart sure as hell didn't either. My mind, on the other hand, had so many thoughts going in and out.

This is going to destroy me, my family, and the world.

I thought to myself.

And before I could sink further into exaggeration, guilt boiled in my chest.

BOOM.

The front door slammed open so hard I panicked.

"TORI!"

Rellik's voice exploded with anger, his facial expression to go along with it.

I barely had time to fix the bed before he stormed in, eyes wild, chest rising and falling like he sprinted through hell's fury to get here.

"Where is he?" Rellik growled. "Tell me, after all these years, you didn't go looking for him."

I froze, the sheet slipping slightly off the bed, heart pounding loudly in my ears. He scanned the room like he was seconds from putting someone through a wall.

I could see outside slightly. Two men were on the porch while three vehicles were parked in the driveway.

"You ditched your protection detail," he barked. "Ghosted John like some rookie. Are you out of your mind?"

"I..." I started, but the words stuck.

"You broke a rule. You know what the hell is going on out there, and you still thought it was smart to disappear and what, go to The South Side?"

His eyes narrowed, locking on the disheveled state around my bed. I saw it hit him. He didn't say a word at first. Just looked away, like the sight of it physically hurt him. Expressing disappointment on his face, exactly as a father would.

"God Damn it, T."

The silence that followed was heavier than anything he could've yelled. It was a disappointment. Fury. Fear.

Then, finally, low and bitter, "You let him in."

It wasn't a question.

I pulled my arms in, almost as if I was ashamed, but quickly snapped out of it. "You don't get to barge in here, judge me, and bring half the North..."

"I do! Especially when your life's on the line, and you're making decisions like this. Tino or not, he's dangerous, and you must know that."

My head quickly turned to a memory of why we call him different names. Valentino was not amused, but we thought it was hilarious. I would say Vale and Rellik would say Tino. And together it was Valentino. We made a gimmick and everything. But those memories are long gone, those laughs will never happen again.

"He's not what you say."

Rellik cut me off with a sharp look. "You think you're the only one who lost him, the guy I considered a brother? You think I haven't lost sleep wondering if I could've done things differently to change how it all ended?" His voice cracked, just for a second. "But brotherhood or not, it doesn't mean you stop seeing the damage they have caused or are capable of."

I looked away.

"You're not just a little girl anymore," he said. "It's just you and me, Mami and Papi are gone. And I will protect you from anything and everyone so you don't feel that pain again. I remember how broken you were after Papi died. I never want to see you like that again."

I squared my shoulders, jaw clenched so tight it ached.

"You think I don't know that?" I said, voice low but steady. "You think I don't feel the pressure every single day to be the version of me you built in your head, the person who is 100% whole and happy?"

Rellik stared at me, that sharp edge in his eyes flickering, surprised, maybe, but still burning.

"I am trying, Rellik," I said. "God, I am trying so fucking hard to be what you want. To play by your rules. To breathe when you say breathe, and stay home when you say. But sometimes I think you forget that I've grown up, and I, too, am a Marcano. *Igual que tú.*"

My chest was heaving now, and I could feel the sting in my eyes.

"Rellik, listen to me. If you continue to plan out my every moment, I will burn your empire down myself. I don't care that half of it is mine." Which technically it was, even though I had no clue what was going on.

The words hit the air like a spark to gasoline. His jaw ticked, but he didn't speak.

"I love you," I added, softer this time. "You mean the world to me. You have done everything in your power to keep me safe, but I need to live my life. Not a life that is overseen by you 24/7."

He didn't respond right away. Just stood there, like he couldn't decide whether to yell or applaud. The silence between us had weight, a history, a bond, an emotional bruise that hadn't quite healed.

"I feel like I can't breathe around you sometimes. I am so afraid to disappoint you," I whispered. "As if I'm being held to a standard I never agreed to. I'm not some distressed damsel, Rellik. Or some pawn that you can control, I snapped, voice rising.

Rellik's jaw flexed. The vein in his temple triggered, but he didn't speak right away. His eyes, the same ones that used to soften when he'd sneak me extra dessert as a kid, were now steel. Cold. Tired. Unforgiving.

"You think this is about control?" he finally growled. "You think I want to smother you? I've spent my whole life keeping you safe. From the streets. From enemies. From truths that would gut you."

"I'm not asking to be coddled," I shot back. "I'm trying to be what you all want, but I'm also me. I'm not made to sit in the corner and wait for permission to breathe."

"That's not what this is."

"Then what is it, Rellik? Why do you act like one wrong move from me will set the whole fucking world on fire?"

He turned away for half a second, dragging a hand over his face, before he spun back toward me. "Because it already did."

I froze.

His voice dropped, low and ragged. "You don't know what he's capable of."

A flash of pain darted through my chest. "Vale?"

He didn't answer. Not at first.

Just repeated himself.

"You disappeared on John. He deflected. "You broke the rule of only staying on the North Side. Do you know how many men I had out last night looking for you?"

"I'm not a child, Rellik."

"No," he snapped. "You're a woman in love with a ghost, or shall I say, Deadman, who should've stayed buried."

My chest heaved. "H-How did you know?"

"How, really?" he spat out. "Because I know the truth, Tori. I'm literally haunted by it. I gave him a lifeline to walk away, but that decision did not come lightly. As long as he was away, it would keep you safe from bearing the weight of the truth. That was the condition. But he couldn't go far enough, could he?"

I stared at him, heart pounding.

Trying to comprehend everything that he is saying.

"You think this is about jealousy or control or me playing big brother?" Rellik's voice cracked, and for the first time, I saw the pain under his fury. "No. This is about you. Because when the truth comes out, when you find out what really happened, your life will fucking crumble, you will be so broken there will be no putting you back together!"

He took a step toward me, voice shaking.

"Do you understand, Tori. I don't know how else I can put it. I am trying to keep you whole, not for me or the Marcano name. For you."

He exhaled hard, but I couldn't move. I couldn't speak.

My throat tightened, my heart pounding so loud it drowned out everything else. But I didn't cry. I didn't fold.

I let the rage consume me.

"YOU! You're the reason he left! You think you're protecting me?" I fired back. "By keeping me in the dark? By not giving me all the information? You're just scared. Scared that if I knew the truth, I'd stop seeing you as the perfect big brother. You're not protecting me, Rellik, you're caging me." Lock me away, place your fucking goons on me. But know this, if I want to be with him, I will. There is no amount of eyes you can put on me that will stop me. All that is going to happen is that they are going to report to you that I DEFIED YOU!"

His jaw clenched. "I'm keeping you alive, can't you see?"

"No," I said, stepping closer. "You're trying to control what you can't fix. You pushed Vale away, WHY? You made him leave. Because he would rather have been with me than a brother to you."

His face twitched. That didn't stop me. I pressed harder. Completely going left.

"What exactly are you covering up. You were the reason I stayed broken for so long. It should have been you who died, not Papi, maybe you..."

That's when it happened.

A crack.

Followed by a sting.

Loud

Sharp.

His hand snapped across my cheek, slightly tipping my right eye with brutal force.

I stumbled, biting my tongue in the process, the taste of pennies flooding my mouth, my balance gone for a second too long.

Silence.

His eyes didn't fill with regret.

He didn't stammer an apology or look horrified.

He just stood there, composed, cold, unapologetic like he'd been waiting for me to cross that line.

Like I deserved it.

Something inside me froze.

Rellik had never laid a hand on me. Not once. Not when I was a reckless teenager. Not even when I screamed and questioned him after Papi died.

 Never.

But he had now.

He turned without another word and walked out, the

door slamming shut behind him like a final judgment.

I don't know how long I stood there. How long I allowed tears to come down my face. My legs eventually moved, but I couldn't feel them. I went completely numb.

I didn't remember how I even got to Rebecca's. My mind was completely blank. I had a bag with me that I couldn't remember packing, and by the time I got to her front door, my cheekbone was already starting to ache.

She opened the door in a silk robe, mid-sentence about the cute foot soldier who walked her out of the club. Then she saw me.

"What in the actual fuck, Tori?" Her voice pierced through my soul.

I didn't say anything.

I just stood there, staring at her, my face throbbing, my body trembling, my thoughts fractured.

She pulled me inside without hesitation, wrapping me in her arms, the way only she knew how.

"He hit me," I said finally, my voice trembling.

"What?" she stated, pulling back to look at me.

"Rellik. He hit me." I swallowed. "He's never hit me."

Her face shifted from shock to fury in seconds, but I couldn't focus on anything except the faded roar in my chest.

Something had changed.

Something had broken.

And I didn't know how to come back from it.

So, I didn't. I just stood there in the living room like a statue while Rebecca quietly locked the door behind us. She didn't ask what happened; she didn't need to. One look at the fresh bruise darkening, and the silence pouring off me was enough.

She took off her boots and stepped toward me, her voice barely above a whisper. "Sit down, T."

"I'm fine," I said, my voice paper-thin.

She gave me a look that could've cut glass. "You've got a bruise on your cheek, and your hands are shaking. You're not fine."

I opened my mouth, ready to argue, but decided it was best to stay closed. There was no point.

Rebecca tugged me gently by the hand and pulled me down onto the couch. She disappeared for a second, then returned with a frozen spoon wrapped in a clean towel and pressed it to my skin.

I flinched.

"Sorry," she said softly. "This'll help with the swelling."

We sat like that for a moment. Quiet. The kind of silence only best friends know how to hold comfortably, but loaded.

Then, as she tucked a throw blanket around me like I was some broken bird, she asked, "He hit you?"

I nodded. Couldn't say it out loud. The lump in my throat was too big.

Rebecca's jaw clenched. "I don't know what the hell is going on between you, Vale, and your brother, but that's not Rellik. Not the one I've known since we were kids. He's a lot of things, controlling, scary, a complete asshole when he's hungry, but he's never put his hands on you."

I looked down at my fingers curled in my lap. "That's what scares me the most."

She let out a breath and leaned her head against mine. "You remember when we were ten, and you broke your wrist trying to jump the fence behind GP Gas & Goods?"

I sniffed.

"Yeah."

"You cried for all of two minutes before Rellik showed up on that stupid skateboard of his, scooped you up, and walked five blocks to the ER without blinking. He was twelve, T. I thought he was going to fight the receptionist for making you wait."

Despite myself, I laughed a little. "Even after getting me in, he dropped the Marcano name to make sure I got the best doctor, and then made fun of me that I was accident-prone."

"Exactly." Her smile faded. "So, what the hell

changed?"

I didn't have an answer.

Rebecca leaned back and studied me for a beat. "Alright. No more serious talk. Let's get ice cream and watch bad movies. I'll even let you wear my ugly cat socks."

I finally looked at her. "You love those socks."

"Yeah, well, I also hate seeing you like this. So, suck it up. Go put them on. And maybe after that we'll go shopping."

"Retail therapy?"

She grinned. "Vengeance in the form of credit card debt. My favorite coping mechanism."

Unfortunately, I did not make it to Rebecca's night of retail therapy. I just sat there with my ice cream and quickly passed out on her couch with my pillow, covered in tears.

The next morning, Rebecca practically shoved coffee into my hand and demanded I put on something cute, but that says 'Not today, asshole.

I gave her a look. "So, black?"

She smirked. "Obviously."

By 8:00 a.m., we were at one of those open-air shopping districts that smelled like overpriced perfume, Chinese food, and poor financial decisions. The sun was bright, the pavement hot beneath our wedges, and the only thing keeping me from curling into a ball was Rebecca dragging me from store to store like a woman on a mission.

"You're going to try this on," she said, holding up a black leather miniskirt and a red top with straps that looked like they'd snap if someone breathed too hard.

I raised an eyebrow. "Is there a full outfit here or just evidence for a future crime scene?"

She grinned. "You said you wanted to feel in control again. First, we begin with the wardrobe."

I rolled my eyes but took the clothes. And I had to admit, once I saw myself in the mirror, dark makeup, messy hair, lips just a little too red, I didn't look like a girl who'd been crying on the floor the night before.

I looked like fire.

Still, something wouldn't settle in my chest. As we moved from one boutique to another, laughing at ridiculous trends and overpriced accessories, I kept pausing, just for a second. A flare of movement caught in the corner of my eye. As if I could feel a shadow that didn't belong there.

It wasn't anything obvious. No lurking figure. No face I recognized.

Just a prickle on the back of my neck. The kind of tension that lives in your bones when your instincts are trying to scream through the noise.

"You good?" Rebecca asked as I froze halfway

between a display of ankle boots and a wall of accessories.

"Yeah." I forced a smile. "Just thought I saw someone."

"You're jumpy." Her tone was light, but I could hear the concern underneath. "You want to head out?"

I shook my head. "No, keep going. I need this."

So, we did. Tried on more clothes. Ate overpriced bagels. Laughed louder than we should've in a quiet store. But every time we stepped outside, the feeling came back.

Similar to eyes pressing into my spine.

As though ghosts were going through my soul every step I took.

And even with Rebecca beside me, even dressed like a girl who'd set the whole city on fire to stay warm, deep down, I felt like prey.

The sun had started to glare by the time we made our way back to the parking garage, arms full of shopping bags and half-melted iced coffees. The kind of late morning where the shadows stretch too long, and the heat finally aims right at you.

"I'm telling you," Rebecca said as we rounded the corner to the garage, "you need to wear that red top to dinner next weekend. If Vale shows up, he will absolutely melt."

I gave her a half-smile. "That's comforting."

But the closer we got to the car, the heavier my legs felt. That feeling hadn't gone away. If anything, it had burrowed deeper. More specific now. Less like paranoia, more like presence.

I glanced over my shoulder. Nothing.

Just the usual bustle of couples walking, people laughing too loudly, the distant hum of an engine turning on somewhere.

But I couldn't shake it.

I started to dwell on this feeling; I was literally giving myself whiplash from how often I kept turning around. Rebecca began to look around, as my best friend.

Rebecca hit the key fob, and the lights on her car blinked in the dim garage.

"You, okay?" she asked again, slower this time.

"Yeah." I lied. "Just fried."

But my hand trembled when I reached for the passenger door.

Because I could still feel it. Eyes. Watching. Measuring. Waiting.

And no matter how many times I told myself it was in my head, it didn't feel like it was.

CHAPTER 5

I couldn't shake the feeling that someone was there in the car with me. It wasn't vague; it was distinct, crawling up my back slowly until the hairs on my neck rose. My shoulders started to tense, alongside my chest tightening.

Was this all in my head?

I held my breath and took a quick peek into the back seat.

Empty.

Obviously.

I let out a trembled sigh. My heart kept pounding as if it knew something that my eyes hadn't been able to capture. I was spiraling, falling down a rabbit hole. This was the kind of shit that happened in horror movies, not in the parking garage of a shopping center.

And yet, the feeling was all too familiar.

Just like in the club.

A shadow that seemed to track my every move.

I felt it in the dressing room. Then, near the makeup counters. Even while I ordered my latte at the cute coffee shop. I kept trying to brush it off, not wanting to ruin our day, but there's only so much pretending

I could do. I blamed it on the stress, the emotional wreckage left over from yesterday. But deep down, I knew better. This wasn't just me being overwhelmed.

This was my soul screaming from the rooftops that something was wrong.

Beside me, Rebecca had already moved on; nothing fazes that girl, I swear. She was digging through her purse, reapplying lip gloss, then unlocking her phone to scroll through social media like we weren't parked in the middle of a slow-brewing nightmare.

My nightmare.

I stared at her.

Nothing.

I stared harder.

Still nothing.

I gave her the most unhinged best-friend glare I could manage, the kind that should've sent needles down her spine. I needed her to snap out of it, now.

"What?" she asked, finally noticing.

"Seriously, get us the fuck out of here," I snapped. "Something doesn't feel right."

She scowled at me, but I guess the way my voice trembled, she knew I was being serious. She shoved her phone back in her purse and started the car.

I took a deep breath, slightly leaned into the

headrest, and closed my eyes.

But something clicked in my head, some survival instinct flaring, and I opened them again.

And there it was.

From the corner of my eye, I caught movement. Headlights shimmered into view, belonging to a black SUV, just a few rows down. It hadn't been there when we parked. I was sure of it. The windows were tinted black, and something about the front of the vehicle was off; I couldn't figure it out. It took me a second.

And then.

"No plate," I muttered.

My eyes narrowed.

I could hear Rellik's voice in my head, giving me a lecture on how to spot dangers around me.

Red Flag.

Even his SUVs had plates front and back

I didn't say anything to Rebecca, not just yet.

She slowly reversed out of the spot and began driving toward the exit. I kept my eyes trained on the SUV, checking the side mirror.

It didn't move, at first.

But just as we reached the exit, it pulled out and turned in our direction.

My stomach dropped.

"Do you see that car?" I asked, keeping my voice low.

Rebecca glanced up. "The SUV?"

"Yeah."

She shrugged, casually. "Probably just circling to pick someone up."

But I couldn't look away.

My eyes were glued.

As we turned out of the plaza, the SUV followed.

Same direction.

Same lane.

Too close for comfort.

We merged onto the main road. It did too.

I straightened up, keeping my eye on the side mirror.

"Okay," I muttered, sarcasm coating my words, "well, that's not suspicious at all."

Rebecca glanced back again, the nervousness now painted clearly across her face. Her usual smile had vanished, replaced with sharp focus. I saw her fingers grip the steering wheel. Tightening.

"Still behind us?" she asked, voice clipped.

"Uh-huh," I whispered.

She went into full driving mode. Switching lanes left and right. Probably not the best time to remind her I get car sick. Well, she'd find out soon enough.

The SUV followed, slower this time compared to the last lane switch. Almost as if they were trying to be less noticeable.

Too late for that.

Ever since I clocked them back in the parking garage. Every move they made now was an instant confirmation that I was right.

My stomach twisted, nerves or motion sickness, who knew, but the anxiety pulsated through my nerves no matter how deep I tried to breathe.

Rebecca's driving got sharper. Reckless, yeah, but she had control. I made a mental note to hire her as my getaway driver if shit ever really hit the fan.

Up ahead, the light was yellow.

Instead of slowing down, she floored it.

"Rebecca!" I shouted, bracing with one hand on the dashboard and the other clutching my seatbelt. I was fully prepared for impact.

"What? Do you want them to catch up?" she snapped.

Obviously not. But I also didn't want to end up on the damn news.

We cleared the intersection by inches. A chorus of honks exploded behind us, and I immediately turned in my seat.

The SUV blasted through the red light like a bat out of hell.

"Um... Becca," I said, barely holding it together.

That's when the panic really set in for both of us.

"What do they want?" we asked at the same time, our voices overlapping.

No answers. Just tight glances between us, her eyes glued to the road, mine glued to the mirror.

They weren't just tailing us.

They were hunting us.

"That's not someone circling to pick someone up," I muttered, my voice tight and low.

Rebecca shot me a sharp look. "Really, now. Okay. Deep breath. We don't know anything for sure."

"Rellik always told me to trust my instincts," I whispered, my voice cracking at the edges. "This isn't good."

Rebecca's eyes darted to me. "Why?"

"Because I had the same feeling the night my dad died," I said. "My gut's never wrong. And you know that."

My heart hammered against my ribs like a warning drum. Every breath felt shallow, tight in my chest. I gripped the door handle with slick palms, cold sweat prickling down my spine. Beside me, Rebecca had her hands tightened on the wheel even more; her palms must be sore and red by now.

The SUV wasn't just following; they were stalking, watching, waiting for the perfect moment to strike.

Every glance in the mirror stabbed me with fresh panic. I wanted to scream at Rebecca, for her to go faster, to do something, but the words stuck in my throat.

This wasn't just fear.

This was survival.

We drove several more blocks, turning down a quieter road, hoping to shake them or at least confirm the truth.

The SUV followed again.

"That's three turns now," Rebecca said. "Still no change."

"Four," I corrected, pulse ringing in my ears. We circled back. "They're still there."

She inhaled sharply. "Shit."

I looked back again, catching a glimpse of the shadowy shape behind the wheel. We were going too fast to see much, just a silhouette leaning forward, studying us, watching us.

"I'm calling Rellik," I said, already unlocking my phone.

It was one of our rules. No matter what, if something went wrong, I had to call him. No questions. No hesitation. I didn't care about what happened yesterday.

I mean, I did. Of course I did. But this?

This trumped everything.

I was scared.

And I needed my brother.

Rebecca didn't say a word this time.

She's usually full of opinions, especially when it comes to Rellik, but now, her silence spoke volumes. She was scared, too. I saw it in the way her jaw clenched as she flipped on the turn signal and veered back onto a busier road, trying to blend into traffic.

Why she was still using signals beat me. Might as well send the SUV a written invitation. Jesus.

I looked back down at my phone.

One ring.

Then straight to voicemail.

"What the fuck," I stammered, my thumb frozen midair. That had never happened before. Ever.

I tried again.

Voicemail.

Again.

Nothing.

"What's going on?" I muttered, jamming Rellik's name over and over like maybe if I hit it hard enough, he'd answer. Was I dialing wrong? Were we out of range? Did this asshole block me when I needed my brother the most?

Rebecca glanced at me, her voice going brittle. "Tori. Why isn't he answering?"

"I don't know."

I really had no clue. And that made everything worse.

I felt clueless. Abandoned. A little more broken than I wanted to admit.

We turned again.

So did they.

This time, closer. Too close.

"I think they're trying to box us in," I said, panic bleeding into my voice. "Drive faster."

"I am." Rebecca's eyes flicked between the mirrors, her breathing shallow. "Shit, Tori..." Her voice cracked under the pressure, and her hands trembled from how hard she had been gripping the wheel.

She slammed the gas pedal, weaving through cars like instinct had fully taken over.

My hands shook in my lap, not because of the SUV.

Because Rellik wasn't answering.

Because the one person who always came through, suddenly wasn't.

And that's when it hit me.

My brother. My shield. The one who once told me I was the only reason he kept the Marcano empire breathing. Decided not to be there for me anymore.

Wouldn't answer.

Maybe didn't care.

I literally didn't know what to do. Rellik was my lifeline.

And then it dawned on me.

There was one lifeline I could reach out to, someone who was just resurrected back into my life.

Someone whose name I'd been too afraid or maybe not even allowed to say out loud just days ago.

"Vale," I murmured, throat tight with emotion.

My hands were shaking, but I didn't hesitate. I swiped past Rellik's name and tapped Valentino.

Thank God he'd put his number into my phone before he left. I never really thought I'd need it, not like this.

One ring.

Half of another.

"Victoria?" His voice was sharp, tense, but present. Immediate.

"Valentino, *ayúdame*. We're being followed," I said, barely steady. "Black SUV. No plates. They've been on us since we left Northgate Plaza. They're not backing off. Vale, I'm scared." My eyes blurred with tears.

The line was quiet, then his voice cut through, fierce and controlled, edged with something darker.

"Stay calm. Don't stop, you hear me? Keep driving."

Beneath the command was something else, anger, maybe even guilt. I could hear him barking orders in the background, controlled yet demanding.

I hated that I had to rely on him. That he was the only one left I could call. But there was no one else.

"I'm sending my guys. They'll intercept. I need to get you somewhere safe."

Just like that, the weight on my chest lifted only slightly, but it was enough to breathe.

"Where?"

"Just trust me. It's a Warehouse on Regal Avenue. Shouldn't be far. The south entrance gate will be open. You're about to cross Dead Mile. Don't stop for anything. I've got eyes on every camera between you and there. I'll guide you."

Vale's voice came through the phone again, sharper now.

"Take the next left after the gas station. Then a quick right at the old firehouse. There's a narrow back road that leads straight to the warehouse. It's not on any main maps. Stay off the main roads as much as possible. I'll talk you through every turn."

Rebecca glanced over, her jaw tight. "What's he saying?"

"He says he has a place we can go. He's sending people."

"I don't trust his people."

"He wouldn't let anything happen to me," I said quietly.

And I meant it.

Whatever mess we were in, whatever past we shared, I knew I could trust him with my life. And I did.

A message pinged.

Vale: *Regal Avenue Warehouse. South entrance. The Gate will be open. Drive straight in, don't stop for anything. You're safe there. I'm watching your every move. Just get to me, Victoria. Please. I can't, if anything happens to you...*

I looked at Rebecca, voice steady despite what I just read.

"Next left after the gas station. Then right at the firehouse. He said there's a hidden back road that leads straight to the warehouse. Stay off the main streets."

Rebecca nodded, her grip not changing a centimeter.

"And he says don't stop," I added. "No matter what."

Rebecca checked the rearview mirror. "They're speeding up."

"I know," I whispered, clutching my phone as if it might anchor me. "But Vale is watching us, and his men should be here soon."

We made a left turn past the gas station. Then the right. The road narrowed, trees closing in on either side.

The headlights behind us flared closer now. Aggressive. Hunting.

My chest clenched, already bracing for impact. My heart pounded so hard it could've cracked the windshield.

Then, all of a sudden.

Three matte-black muscle cars appeared out of nowhere.

One slid in behind the SUV. Another dropped behind us, a wall of steel and motion. The third surged into place in front of us, taking the lead like it had done this a hundred times.

Vale's voice returned, lower and tighter now.

"That's them in front of you. Follow their lead. Don't fall behind."

The SUV behind us slowed, boxed them in, and cut

us off. I watched it fade into the distance, smaller...
smaller... gone.

Ahead, a massive warehouse door rolled open.

"There," I said. "That's it."

Rebecca didn't hesitate. Tires shrieked as she floored
it, launching us into the open bay.

The second we stopped, the doors slammed shut
behind us.

Silence.

Not peaceful. Not still.

It was the kind of silence that hums with warning,
charged, electric, the pause before everything
changes.

I exhaled for the first time in minutes, dragging
shaky air into my lungs.

My wedges hit the concrete floor as I stepped out,
the sound echoing through the vast space.

Rebecca followed, clutching her purse like it might
get stolen right in front of her.

The warehouse was a completely different world.

 The air inside was cool, almost sterile, nothing like
the heat and chaos of the chase. Overhead lights
flickered on one by one, causing my eyes to follow
them, casting long shadows across the concrete
floor, exposing every crack. The faint hum of engines
and low voices echoed like ghosts in the

monumental space. I could smell oil, dust, and something faintly metallic.

Vale's men moved with quiet purpose, their eyes sharp. Everything here was controlled, calculated, a stark contrast to the frantic fear we had just escaped.

Shadows crawled across the high ceilings, broken only by a single beam of light that stretched just far enough to find him.

My eyes locked with his.

Valentino.

And just like that, the fear in my veins turned into something else entirely.

I was glad there was distance between us, because the moment our eyes met, I knew I blushed. I could hear the whispers in the background, hushed and curious. Who was I? What I meant.

He stood in the middle of the warehouse like every war I'd ever survived and every comfort I'd ever lost.

His eyes never left mine, but slowly, they began to drift. Down. Studying. Devouring.

Relief flickered across his face for a fraction of a second, until I stepped into the light.

His gaze caught on the bruise.

The one blooming dark and furious across my cheekbone.

The one I had entirely forgotten about during this

whole ordeal.

His entire body stiffened. The relief vanished from his face, replaced with something darker. Something dangerous.

He didn't speak. He didn't need to.

He walked toward me with steady, lethal intent.

When he reached me, he lifted my chin gently, too gentle for the fire burning behind his eyes. His thumb grazed just beneath the bruise, the lightest touch.

A prayer.

A promise.

A threat.

"Who did this?"

His voice was gravel-soaked in gasoline.

"Vale."

"Don't," he growled, "who the fuck put their hands on you?"

I opened my mouth. Closed it.

I didn't answer. I didn't have to.

My silence said everything.

Behind me, Rebecca shifted.

"Okay," she said cautiously, voice too bright to be

natural, "so just going to throw it out there, anyone else feel like we stepped into an action movie?"

Vale didn't even blink. His focus didn't move an inch.

Rebecca cleared her throat. "Right. Cool. I'll just be over here not getting shot."

She backed away slowly, giving us space, but not before shooting me a glance that screamed: *Wow, he's changed. No wonder you're a hot mess.*

Vales's jaw clenched.

"Victoria."

My name was a warning now, spoken low and rough, like a fuse waiting for a match.

"Tell me. Now."

I looked down, straight at the floor. Still refusing to answer.

"Rellik."

He didn't say it like a guess.

He said it like a verdict.

"That mother…" Vale's jaw snapped shut as his breath hitched. "He knows what this means."

He snapped his fingers.

Two of the Kings stepped forward like ghosts peeling from the shadows, silent, deadly, waiting.

"Every one of his places," Vale said, voice like cut glass. "His bars. His poker rooms. Fuck, even his lieutenants. I want them in ruins by sunrise."

"Valentino, stop." I grabbed his arm.

He didn't flinch. Didn't even look at me.

When he finally turned, his eyes were wildfire.

"You don't get it, do you?" he said, voice low and shaking with restraint. "No one touches my Queen."

His words hung in the air as a claim, a promise, a threat.

"You think it's just some title?" he continued, his voice breaking at the edges. "Believe it or not, Victoria, you are the Queen of the South Side Kings. These men would die for me, die for you, for us. That's what you mean to me. Nobody touches you. Nobody touches the Queen."

My breath caught.

"Not your brother. Not your past. Not fate," he said. "Anyone who lays a hand on you answers to me."

He turned back to his men, fire in every step.

"I want him to feel it," he snarled. "I want him to know the cost of marking my Queen."

Valentino wasn't just angry; he was a man who was possessed. This wasn't rage coming out of nowhere; it was a reckoning. Years of betrayal and heartbreak that had been festering beneath the surface, and now they were spilling out in fire and ash. He barked orders with the weight of blood-soaked history. I saw something flicker in his eyes, a memory, maybe, of the last time he and Rellik faced off. Blood. Ruin. Regret.

His men didn't question him. They just moved, loyal, lethal, and ready to burn the world down for their King.

"I'm not a pawn in your war with him," I hissed, voice cracking despite myself.

He stepped toward me again, and this time, his heat wrapped around me like a blanket.

His touch was both gentle and fierce as he brushed the hair from my face. His eyes looked me up and down like he was trying to memorize every scar I carried, visible and hidden. I wanted to scream at him, to push him away, but the raw vulnerability in his gaze stopped me.

"You're not a pawn," he said, voice low and steady. "You're everything."

The words hit me like a punch and a promise all at once. I wanted to believe him. I needed to. But trust wasn't something that came easily, not with him, not now.

"You were never a pawn," he said quietly. "You're the whole fucking board. And I will burn every piece before I let anyone put you in check ever again."

I couldn't speak. I just stared at him, chest heaving.

Vale exhaled, his voice softening. He reached up,

slightly moving my hair to the side while giving me the most intimate kiss behind my neck.

"You're safe here," he said, quieter now. "My men will cover every corner. No one gets in. Not even him."

Behind me, Rebecca was silent. I could feel her watching, her jaw probably still on the floor after Vale announced my title, but I couldn't tear my eyes away from him. From the storm still raging behind him.

And in that moment, bruised, shaken, furious, I realized something terrifying.

Vale wasn't just angry.

He was ready for war.

He didn't say another word after that.

Just a sharp nod to one of the guys standing in the shadows.

Rebecca cleared her throat, breaking the charged silence.

"I'll just give you two some privacy," she said softly, her voice steady but careful.

Her eyes flicked between us, reading the fire still crackling between Valentino and me, before she took a small step back.

"Text me if you need me," she added, forcing a half-smile that didn't quite reach her eyes.

Then she turned and disappeared into the shadows of the warehouse, leaving the space heavy with unspoken words and electric tension.

Vale gave one of his men a motion with his hand. I had no clue what it meant, but they clearly did.

The far side of the warehouse began to hum with life as overhead lights flickered on, casting a soft amber glow over the concrete floor. Then came the sound of an engine rolling forward. Smooth. Controlled. Powerful.

And then I saw it.

The car.

I forgot to breathe, just stood there like a deer caught in the headlights. Almost literally.

A Mercedes-Benz S-Class, sleek and black as midnight, glides out of the shadows like a ghost. But it wasn't just the car; it was the details. The custom interior was trimmed in the most elegant, soft gold leather, glowing under the light like a secret only I was meant to know.

My hands trembled.

"I said this once," I whispered, voice tight in my throat. "I was fifteen, and you asked me if I could have anything in the world, what would it be. I told you this. This exact car. Black exterior, gold trim. I said it looked like royalty with a hint of peace."

And then it clicked.

Royalty.

The name of the Kings. Where it all came from.

He didn't move.

He just watched me. That same gaze that always saw more than I wanted it to.

"You remembered?" I muttered, avoiding eye contact.

"I never forgot," he said quietly. "Even when I tried to."

I stepped closer, fingers hovering just above the door handle like I was scared it might disappear. When I opened it, the interior light glowed softly and golden, like candlelight. There it was, gold-stitched seats, polished trim, even the same scent I used to dream about, warm leather and vanilla. Like the kind of life I thought I'd never get to live.

"You really had it built like this?"

Vale nodded once. "Every single detail. It took a long time, but I also made sure to get it right. You said this car made you feel like your future could be beautiful, even when everything else felt like shit."

I turned to face him, the weight of it all crashing into my chest like a wave. This was so much all at once.

"You can't just show up and hand me something like this," I whispered. "Something I dreamt about before the world went to crap."

He stepped closer. "I can when it's for you."

I shut my eyes just for a second, trying to fight the

sting building behind them.

"You think this car and your proclamation of who I am to The Kings makes things right?"

"No," he said. "But maybe it reminds you, I was always listening. Always loving you. Even when I wasn't near you."

God, the way he said it. As if it hurt him or cost him something.

"You're out of your mind," I muttered, a smirk ghosting across my lips.

He smiled faintly. "Probably. But know that I'm yours."

I sank into the driver's seat. The scent hit me first, warm leather and vanilla, a perfume of dreams I'd almost forgotten. My fingers traced the gold stitching on the seat; every stitch had meaning, soft and perfect beneath my touch. Each detail whispered some secret late nights, moments stolen before the world went dark.

Sitting inside felt like stepping into a memory I'd never dared to hold onto.

This wasn't just a car.

It was hope wrapped in black and gold.

A fragile promise that maybe, just maybe, the future could still be beautiful.

Just like I always said, it could be.

Valentino walked around to the passenger side and sat down beside me, silent. His presence filled the space effortlessly, as if it had always been the plan. As if the road ahead already belonged to us.

The doors clicked shut, sealing us in.

I glanced at him from the corner of my eye. "You going to tell me where we're going?"

He looked at me, slow and serious. "Somewhere safe. Somewhere you can breathe. Then, softer, "I'll guide you. I know you'll want to drive."

The way he said it made my chest tighten, not just for the promise of safety, but for the weight of everything we hadn't said. Everything he still wasn't saying.

But for now, I didn't ask. I didn't push.

I just put the car in drive and pressed the gas pedal.

We pulled out of the warehouse, the sunshine hitting the hood just right. The world felt quieter with him beside me, causing the kind of calm that thrums just beneath the skin, charged, unspoken, and dangerous.

I didn't know where we were headed, and frankly, I didn't care.

But as the road opened up and his hand found mine on the center console, steady and grounding, I let myself believe, just for a second, that maybe this time we weren't heading toward disaster.

Maybe this time, we were chasing something worth

surviving for.

CHAPTER 6

I shouldn't feel this scared.

Especially when I am in the car with Valentino by my side.

I know his scent, his touch, the cadence of his breathing, and still, I can't shake the feeling that we're being watched.

Whoever was in that SUV earlier has clearly gotten under my skin. But his men must've handled it by now. Right?

Still, I keep glancing behind us, my fingers tracing the stitching on the seat, each loop of thread grounding me just enough to keep from spiraling.

And then—I see it.

A black SUV.

Again.

And again.

"We passed that same black SUV twice," I say softly.

"I noticed," he answers, not taking his eyes off the road. "They're not following us anymore. We lost them back on Moore Rd."

"But you saw it?"

"I always see it, Victoria."

His voice is calm but clipped, protective in the way that feels like a warning. I press my lips together and nod, pretending that's enough to settle the sick weight in my stomach.

Still, the unease clings to me like static. "Could've been one of Rellik's guys. It could've been someone else. I don't know anymore."

Valentino doesn't respond right away, and that silence is louder than any siren.

"Rellik's men don't tail people sloppily," he finally says. "And if it were mine, I'd know. Which leaves a third option."

I turn to him. "You think someone else is watching me?"

He exhales through his nose, eyes narrowing. "I think someone wants you to feel watched. That's a message."

My blood runs cold. "Why?"

"We'll talk at the office."

"Why not now?"

He glances at me, something unreadable in his eyes. "Because you're not safe yet."

Those words should terrify me.

But somehow, the way he says them, low and certain, makes me feel more protected than I want to admit.

I keep driving, my jaw tight, nerves buzzing. He notices. Of course he does. He reaches out.

A quiet, calming touch.

His hand settles on my thigh, slow, steady, warm.

And I hate that it helps. That just one touch from him can silence every screaming thought in my head. I hate that a part of me still trusts him with things I don't even trust myself to name.

The building comes into view, glass and steel rising out of the city like it has something to prove.

Valentino motions for me to pull into the underground garage, and for a second, the only sound is the low hum of the engine winding down.

We step into the elevator from the parking level, just the two of us in the mirrored box. I keep my arms crossed, fingers digging into my sides like I can keep my thoughts from spilling out.

"Do you think it was the cartel?" I ask finally.

He doesn't answer immediately. He presses the button for the lobby, then leans back against the wall, his jaw tightening. "If it were the cartel, they wouldn't follow. They'd act."

That doesn't make me feel better. If anything, it chills me more.

The elevator doors open into a quiet lobby. Sterile. Empty. The security guard gives us a nod, as if he's been trained not to ask questions. Valentino doesn't pause. He guides me to the second elevator, the private one.

We step inside.

The doors close.

He pulls a key from his pocket and slides it into the slot, unlocking the button for the top floor.

"You think someone's sending a message," I say. "But to whom? Me, you, Rellik?"

He exhales slowly, sharply. "Does it matter?"

"Yes. It matters to me if I'm caught in someone's crosshairs because of either of you."

He flinches just barely.

"I don't know who it was," he says. "But the way they moved, the timing, it wasn't random. This wasn't about you being beside me."

"What do you mean?"

He looks at me, really looks this time. "I mean, they knew it would shake you. And that I'd react."

My heart drops. "So, they were watching both of us?"

"Maybe. Or maybe it was just for you."

I lean back against the cool elevator wall, my breath catching. "You said it wasn't your men. And it wasn't my brother's. So, who the hell would want to scare me like that?"

The elevator dings. Top floor.

Valentino pulls out the key.

He steps forward but doesn't walk out. Instead, he turns to me, voice low.

"There's one possibility that makes the most sense. Someone who knew what you meant to me then. Someone who knows what power I hold now, and you're the only way to get to me."

My stomach twists.

"Who?"

He doesn't answer.

He doesn't need to.

His silence speaks louder than any name could.

Someone from his past.

Someone who never forgot what I was to him.

But how would they even know? I barely found out that Rellik knew.

"Victoria," he starts, gently. "Before we go inside, I need you to understand something."

I met his eyes.

"This, it's not random. Whoever's watching you, they've been waiting. Calculating. Patient."

Valentino puts his foot so the elevator doors stay open, revealing a long hallway lined with glass and marble, too sterile and quiet. He steps forward, but I don't move.

My feet won't budge.

My body says no, even though my mind is screaming for logic.

I've survived years under Rellik's rules. I don't fall apart. I don't panic.

So why now?

Maybe because everything's happened too fast.

Vale is back in my life.

Rellik and I aren't speaking.

I'm being followed.

And who knows what's unraveling on the North Side?

What if this isn't just some ghost from Vale's past?

What if it is Rellik testing me?

Or worse, warning me?

You don't know what he's capable of, Rellik said.

What if I walk into this office and come out in a body bag?

I feel the walls closing in. My pulse thumps loudly in my ears, and I can't hear anything else. Every footstep echoes like a gunshot. Every security camera feels like an unblinking eye trained on me. I feel stripped, exposed like someone's already marked me.

I clutch my arms across my chest, like I can trap the panic before it breaks open.

"Vic...?" Vale's voice cuts through the fog. It's calm, but laced with concern now.

He turns around, holding the doors once again, eyes locking on me.

I shake my head, stumbling back half a step.

"This was a mistake. I shouldn't have come. What if someone followed us? What if they know where I live? What if this is just part of something bigger and I'm just..."

"Victoria."

His voice slices through the panic like a blade. Sharp. Commanding.

Knowing that nobody else calls me that is my weakness.

And when I meet his eyes, I see it.

That look.

The same one from years ago that used to make my breath catch.

The one that told me I was the center of his world and the edge of his destruction.

"I can't breathe," I whisper.

He closes the distance in two steps.

"Victoria, look at me."

I do.

And before the next frantic thought can even form, before the next breath can collapse in my chest, he kisses me.

Not softly.

Not sweetly.

But completely.

His hand slides behind my neck, anchoring me as his mouth claims mine with a kind of desperation that says, *You're here. You're safe. You're mine.*

The panic crumbles.

The noise fades.

All that's left is heat, memory, and the taste of something I never honestly forgot.

My hands, traitorous and wild, in the fabric of his jacket. I don't know if I'm pulling him closer or trying to keep myself from falling.

Maybe both.

Maybe I'm still that girl who never stopped waiting for him to come back.

Even when I swore, I hated him.

When he finally pulls away, my lips feel swollen. My

heart's still racing, but not from fear anymore.

"Still can't breathe?" he murmurs, his thumb brushing across my cheek.

I glare at him. "That was manipulative."

He smirks. "You're welcome."

I shove his chest. He catches my wrist before I can turn away, gentle but firm.

"Victoria," he says, voice quiet. Steady. Dangerous with intention.

"I'm not letting anything happen to you. Not this time."

That promise sits between us like a live wire.

Whether I believe him or not.

I stepped into this building.

I'm in it now.

And so is he.

We walk down the hallway together.

He opens the office door and steps aside so I can walk in first.

It's colder than I expected, sleek concrete floors, tall windows stretching up like cathedral glass, and that ever-present scent of sharp cologne and something darker I can't name. His presence is everywhere.

Expensive.

Controlled.

Commanding.

I walk in slowly, unsure of whether to sit or pace.

 I choose neither.

Vale closes the door behind us with a soft click, and the lock slides into place like a final decision.

"I meant what I said," he says behind me. "No one touches you. Ever again."

I turn around slowly.

The adrenaline hasn't left me; it's curdled into something heavier.

Hotter.

My chest is still tight, but now it's for a different reason.

He walks toward me, unhurried.

"I am not strong enough to stay away," he says.

I tilt my chin up, defiant, even as everything in me trembles.

"You don't get to make promises like that," I whisper. "Not after disappearing. Not after ghosting me. Not after making me wonder if I was just some mistake."

His jaw clenches.

"You were never a mistake," he says through gritted

teeth. "And I never ghosted you."

I want to believe him. God, I do.

But I'm tired

Tired of speaking in circles.

Tired of begging for the truth.

Tired of pretending the heat between us doesn't still pulse like a fuse lit too long ago.

I cross the room and grab his face, and I kiss him.

Fierce.

Desperate.

Starved.

It's not careful. It's not sweet.

It's six years of silence and pain and longing crashing into one violent, beautiful kiss.

His hands are on me in seconds, one sliding up my thigh, the other tangling in my hair. I feel the edge of his desk hit the backs of my legs.

He lifts me onto it without breaking the kiss, spreading my knees as he steps between them.

"Vale," I breathe against his mouth, "tell me this isn't just some power trip. Tell me you still feel it."

He growls low, primal. Something pulled straight from the place where he buried us.

"I feel everything, Victoria. I never stopped. I'm trying to show you that."

My hands tear at his jacket, his shirt, anything I can find. I don't want distance. I don't want words.

I wrap my legs around his hips, locking him in.

His mouth trails down my neck as I arch back, the cold wood biting into my spine.

The sun shining through the windows, exposing us.

He tears open my blouse like it offended him.

My fingers fumble at his belt, his zipper, desperate and clumsy. He helps.

With one hand, he unthreads the belt from his pants in one practiced motion. Then, slowly, he loops the tail back through the buckle, forming a figure eight.

His eyes hold mine as he places my wrist inside.

"Trust me?" he asks, voice rough with restraint.

I nod.

He bites down on the end of the belt to tighten the loop, securing my wrists together, then lifts my bound hands over my head, just long enough to free himself.

And then he's pressing against me like he can't bear another second apart.

The first thrust knocks the air from my lungs.

I gasp, wanting to hold onto him.

He sets a rhythm that is rough, fast, and unrelenting.

Like he's trying to erase time.

As if he's trying to remind my body who it belonged to first.

He wraps my arms around him, locking us together.

Our breath mingles in broken sobs and moans.

His name leaves my lips like a prayer, a curse, a confession.

"Vale."

His forehead presses to mine.

"Say it again."

"Valentino, please."

He drives deeper, groaning against my mouth.

 His hands grip my thighs, anchoring us both in this collision of pain and pleasure.

Every thrust feels like a claim.

Every kiss is like a promise.

We come undone together loud, raw, real.

And when the last wave crashes, I cling to him, chest to chest, breath for breath, heart to heart.

We stay like that, tangled, silent, shaking on the desk where empires are probably planned, where lies were told.

Where he just made love to me like he was dying.

And maybe he was.

Because I think a part of both of us just came back to life.

We're still tangled together, his chest rising and falling against mine, my back pressed against the cool surface of his desk.

The office is quiet now, safe from the sound of our breathing. That raw energy between us has simmered into something slower, deeper. My fingers rest on his chest, tracing a slow circle as he brushes a strand of hair from my face.

He presses his lips to my forehead and gives me a soft kiss before resting his chin on the crown of my head.

Neither of us spoke for a moment.

I don't know whether I'm afraid to break the silence or want to live in it a little longer. Safe in this moment. In him. I was so tired of arguing, tired of pain. Maybe letting go wasn't a weakness. Perhaps it was survival. Should I forget the past and move forward?

Could Valentino be my future?

Then he says softly, "There's something I want you to come to tonight."

I shift slightly, pulling back enough to look at him. "What kind of something?"

"A benefit. High-profile. Politicians. Business heads. A few families from out of town." His thumb strokes my hip. "And I want you with me. On my arm."

My brows lift, amused. "Since when do I do black-tie events?"

"You don't," he says with a smirk. "Yet. But you will. You belong there, Victoria. I want everyone to see that. They know the face of the King. It's time they see the face of the most beautiful Queen."

There's something in his eyes I don't quite recognize. Not just pride. Not just possession. There's vulnerability there, like he's asking for more than just a night, like he's asking me to step into his world again and stay.

"I'll send a car for you at seven," he adds, brushing his lips against mine. "And before you argue, yes, I'm insisting."

I sigh, pretending to roll my eyes, even though my heart's already thudding. "What should I wear?"

His smile deepens. "Something that makes it hard for me to keep my hands off you."

"You say that like anything wouldn't qualify."

He laughs under his breath, pulling me closer one last time before helping me off the desk. We fix ourselves up in silence, straightening clothes, smoothing hair, but there's an unspoken shift between us now. A line crossed. A door opened. It was as if we let everything go and just decided to be happy.

He drives me home, the car ride quiet but warm, his hand resting on my thigh like a calm promise.

When we pull up to my building, he leans in and murmurs, "Seven, Victoria. Make sure you're ready."

I nod, too breathless to say anything back.

The second I walk into my apartment, I let out a sound I didn't even know I was holding in.

A nervous laugh. Something between panic and happiness.

He waited, just like before, engine purring until I was safely inside. Only then does he pull away.

I lean against the door, heart racing. Smiling like an idiot. It was like I was eighteen all over again, back when he used to flirt shamelessly and check up on me behind Rellik's back. But this felt different.

This time, he wasn't hiding.

He was doing it.

He wants me there.

In his world.

On his arm.

No more secrets. No more shadows. Just like he promised six years ago.

I head straight to my closet, already scanning through dresses I haven't worn in years. I tried on three in rapid succession; each one was tossed onto my bed with growing frustration.

Too tight. Too flashy. Too plain. Too safe.

Do I look like I belong?

Do I even want to?

Rebecca's voice flashes in my head. *You're the Latina Marilyn Monroe, babe, just own it.*

I stare at myself in the mirror. Trying to see that version of me. The one who doesn't flinch. The one who walks into a room as if she owns it, not like she's bracing for a fight.

I can't tell if I'm shaking from nerves or something more profound. But one thing's for sure, tonight is going to change everything.

I'm mid-rampage through my closet hangers clattering, zippers zipping, me muttering to myself like a lunatic when I hear a knock.

Soft. Barely audible.

I freeze.

Another knock. Then her voice, unmistakable.

"Tori, open up. I brought wine and judgment."

I practically sprint to the door and yank it open. There stands Rebecca, in leggings and a cropped hoodie, hair half up, and eyes already full of commentary. She's holding a bottle of red in one hand and a medium-sized black box in the other.

"What's that?" I ask.

"This?" She says dramatically, holding it up like it might contain a cursed object, "It was sitting on your front mat like it was waiting to be kidnapped. No name. Just you. Obviously, I opened the outer box to make sure it wasn't a bomb."

She waltzes inside without waiting for an invite, of course, and sets everything down on the kitchen counter.

I shut the door behind her, suddenly breathless again.

My name is handwritten across the top of the box.

Victoria.

In clean, dark script.

Only one person calls me that.

My fingers tremble slightly as I untie the satin ribbon, heart hammering harder with every pull.

Inside was a gown.

Midnight blue, rich and almost black in dim lighting. The fabric is satin with just enough structure to hug every curve without clinging too tightly. The neckline is a classic off-the-shoulder sweetheart cut, soft, romantic, but commanding attention. The bodice is corseted, giving shape and strength, and the skirt flows down into a dramatic A-line with a thigh-high slit that promises danger and elegance in equal measure.

It's timeless. Bold.

Everything he sees in me, even when I don't.

Beneath the tissue paper, a folded note.

I read it once.

Then again, slower.

You once told me that you always wanted to feel like a princess going to a ball. I hope this helps you feel like that tonight.

No signature. Just that.

But it hits me so hard I have to sit.

Rebecca, suddenly realizing this isn't just some cute online find, leans over my shoulder.

"Damn," she breathes. "That man is playing chess while everyone else is tossing Uno cards."

I laugh, but my throat feels tight.

My finger retraces the paper, like touching the words might make them more real.

It was something I'd told him years ago after a party where everyone brushed past me like I was nothing more than Rellik's quiet little sister. I'd stood there in a plain dress, invisible, while the world spun around me.

I just wanted to feel acknowledged. To feel like the most beautiful girl in the room, for once.

I didn't think he even remembered.

But he did.

He remembered me.

He keeps telling me he never forgot, and maybe it's time I start believing him.

Rebecca places the wine down and pulls the gown out with reverence. "Okay, Queen. You are wearing this. Period. No argument. Take a shower. We've got hair to curl, lashes to glue, a bruise to cover up, and your anxiety to manage."

I'm still holding the note, my thumb brushing the curve of his handwriting.

And somewhere deep in my chest, something cracks open.

Something I've kept locked away for years.

Hope.

Real, terrifying, beautiful hope.

After the shower, she got to work. One thing after another. It took time, but we were done.

Rebecca gives me one last approving glance, her purse already swinging on her arm. "Tori, he's going to lose his damn mind when he sees you. And if he doesn't, give me five minutes alone with him and I'll knock some sense into that beautiful skull of his."

I laugh, but nerves creep up my spine like cold fingers. "Thanks, Bec. For everything."

"I'll see you tomorrow if you survive," she adds with

a wink before slipping out the door.

"Too soon," I mutter, giving her a bitchy expression as the door clicks shut.

6:55 p.m.

I gave myself one last glance in the mirror, smoothing the gown over my hips, adjusting the strap on my shoulder. My makeup was soft but confident, lips touched with a warm nude gloss, eyes defined just enough to look effortless. Vale would notice every detail; I was sure of it.

I inhaled slowly, letting the feeling sink in. I looked beautiful. Not cute. Not decent. Not passable.

Beautiful.

I hadn't felt like this in years. Not since before everything fell apart. And now, someone had chosen this dress just for me. Had remembered my favorite color. Had written me a note that only *I* could understand.

Valentino had seen me and not just the version I gave the world, but the real me underneath it all.

And he wanted me by his side.

Clutching my small purse close to my body, I stepped out of my apartment and into the dusky evening. The air smelled faintly of jasmine and asphalt. My heels clicked gently against the concrete, and for a moment the world felt quiet, as if it were holding its breath with me.

Then I saw it.

The black car.

Sleek, polished, waiting at the end of the street like a promise kept. One of his men stood outside the passenger door, arms folded, posture casual but alert.

I smiled. I actually smiled.

For the first time in a long, long time, I felt wanted. Not tolerated. Not protected like some fragile porcelain doll.

Wanted. Desired. Seen.

And just as that feeling settled into my chest.

A white van skidded around the corner.

Fast.

Too fast.

Before I could turn, before I could even scream, the side door flew open.

Hands.

Rough. Rushed. Covered in leather and sweat.

One clamped over my mouth.

Another around my waist.

My purse fell.

I thrashed, kicked, punched, and bit, but they didn't flinch.

"Queen V!"

A voice shouted from the black car. Doors slammed.

Gunfire cracked like fireworks.

But it was too late.

I was already inside.

The van door slammed shut behind me, drowning out the chaos.

I felt the jolt of acceleration. Tires squealed. The city blurred past the narrow slits of the window as I was pulled further into the dark.

They had me.

And Vale...

He didn't.

Elsewhere - Valentino's office

His phone rang. A number he knew.

"¿Qué pasa?"

Silence. Then breathing. Heavy. Shaken.

Finally, a voice.

"We lost her."

Everything in Vale stilled.

"What do you mean you lost her?"

"She was taken. White van. We got a few rounds in, but they vanished. It was clean. Too clean."

His knuckles turned white around the phone.

"Lock everything down. I want every camera pulled, every contact reached, and every man we've got on the street."

A pause. His voice dropped low. Deadly.

"I want her back. Now!

CHAPTER 7

The van jerked violently as it blew right through a red light, tires screeching beneath us. My body slammed into the wall before I could brace myself, breath catching, heart pounding so hard I thought it might stop entirely.

You would think they would at least buckle me in, try to keep me in one piece.

Gunshots still rang in my ears, distant but echoing inside my skull like they were bouncing off the walls of my memory.

I try to compile my thoughts, trying hard not to panic.

Did I hear them call me *Queen V*?

I couldn't even process it. Not with my wrists bound. Not with fear clawing its way up my body, spreading like wildfire. Not with my world spiraling into chaos behind tinted glass.

But why would they even yell that?

Did Vale tell them to?

Was he right that these men would do anything to protect me?

Or.

No, that didn't make sense.

Why would protection feel like an ambush? Why drag me off the street like some target?

But then I remembered their faces.

They weren't cold.

They weren't cruel.

They looked worried, genuinely concerned. For me.

My breath caught again, sharp and shaky.

I shook my head and forced myself to get back to now.

"What the hell is happening?" I gasped, struggling against the restraints. My voice trembled, tears hot and steady on my cheeks. I hated how small it sounded. Usually, I am the loud one, the opinionated one. But now I was the victim.

Outside, the city lights flashed past buildings, headlights, shadows, but none of it mattered. My panic didn't care about any of it.

I heard voices. The masked driver barked something over his shoulder. I couldn't make out the words, but the tone was urgent. One of the men in the back responded in a low, clipped, and annoyed voice.

The same man who'd grabbed me.

The one with the black tactical vest, the mask, the gloves over my mouth.

The one who slammed the van door shut behind me.

And then it hit me.

The voice.

The scent.

The grip on my arms was rough, but familiar.

These weren't strangers.

These weren't enemies.

They were his.

My breath came faster now, shallow and erratic.

I didn't know if I should be relieved or more afraid.

Rellik's men.

He sent them for me.

A slow chill crept through me. "Oh my God."

The realization that my own brother was behind this was like a slap in the face, again.

Of course, he found out. About the South Side. About Vale. About the damn event. He'd seen the cameras, heard the whispers.

Queen of the South Side.

His sister.

The ultimate betrayal.

He didn't call.

Didn't warn me or give me an ultimatum.

Didn't even yell.

He just sent his men.

"Pathetic," I muttered.

As if I were nothing. Not family. Not blood. Just another mistake to clean up.

I leaned my head back, closed my eyes, and tried to breathe. It didn't work. The hurt settled deeper, buried behind my ribs, where nothing could reach it, where even Vale couldn't pull it free.

Was Rellik really that petty? That childish? As if Vale had stolen his favorite toy, and now he was throwing a fucking tantrum?

I turned toward the window and froze.

King Street.

South Side*?*

The sharp edges of the city lit up under neon lights, casting reflections over the tinted glass like fractured ghosts. My breath caught in my throat.

Why the hell would they go through here?

Where were they taking me?

Or worse, was this just an ego move?

Some sick, subtle way to prove they could drive straight through Vale's side of the city and still not save me. To show me how alone I really was.

I would have never thought Rellik would do such a thing, but then again, I never thought he would have ever hit me either.

A jolt of adrenaline hit my gut as soon as we passed *La Corona.*

Where it all started, from then on, I noticed each street that we passed.

We were so close.

Vale's territory. If I could scream loud enough, kick hard enough.

If someone just looked up.

No.

I wasn't getting out of this van.

I wasn't going to that event.

My dress was already ruined.

My life, probably next.

I wasn't going anywhere except wherever Rellik wanted me to.

My chest ached not just from fear, but from something heavier, like betrayal.

He didn't even let me choose.

He just took me.

Why couldn't we talk this out? Does he truly hate Valentino so much that he would rather I rot in whatever place he has ready for me?

I pressed my head to the cool metal wall and stared out as the South Side lights disappeared behind us, crushed under the weight of distance and deceit.

What felt like forever passed. Finally, the van slowed and turned onto a narrow, unlit road. Palm Trees lined the street, eerie in the dark. A gated house sat ahead, quiet, isolated. Not one of Rellik's usual crash pads. I heard the gate's weight as it screeched open. As the driver exited the van, I heard him call out to someone.

Then the side door slid open, and I froze.

"John?"

He wouldn't meet my eyes.

"John," I said again, louder this time, feeling my voice shake with disbelief.

"I'm sorry, Tori," he murmured, eyes on the floor. "I didn't know until the last minute. I... I have to follow orders."

His voice was thick with guilt. But the other guy had no hesitation. His grip on my arm was rough, impersonal. A soldier moving a pawn.

"Let me go!" I shouted, kicking out. "You don't have to do this! You don't know what you're starting!"

"You don't understand," John said, his voice tight, almost pleading. "Rellik found out about the South Side, about the event. They're calling you Queen V. Then the attacks started to happen, Tori. Iron Grave is up in flames as we speak. He panicked."

I froze, the words hitting harder than they should've.

Some of these things, they were happening because of me.

Because I crossed the line. Because I didn't stay quiet. Because I saw Vale.

My decisions were starting fires.

Literally.

But it still didn't give him the right.

"That's no excuse to kidnap me!" I spat every syllable laced in venom.

There she is. I thought to myself.

He winced.

Good.

They dragged me up a narrow walkway.

I stumbled once, then again, but they didn't slow down.

The house had no sense of warmth to it.

It felt like the kind of place where people were tortured for information, where screams were heard and ignored.

The walls were stained a sickly yellow, nicotine bleeding into every crack like the men here smoked through every hour of every day. The air was stale, heavy with old sweat and something else I couldn't name. I caught sight of takeout containers piled on the tables, greasy bags, half-eaten boxes, and a rotting smell beneath it all.

A safe house?

Really?

Was that what this was supposed to be?

My thoughts spiraled, at war with themselves again.

Was I wrong about everything?

Was Rellik doing this because he thought he was protecting me?

Super, I thought bitterly. Stockholm Syndrome with a side of family trauma.

The room they pushed me into was stripped down and silent. It was just one window, pitch black, so I couldn't look outside. No clock. No way to track time. Just a bed, a chair, a dresser, and four walls that seemed to close in a little tighter with every breath.

"Wait, don't do this," I begged, locking eyes with John. "You know this isn't right."

His jaw clenched. "I have to inform Rellik that you're here. Just stay put for now."

Then the door shut.

And I was alone.

Click. Followed by the sound of a key turning to secure the lock.

I didn't move at first. Just stood there in my navy dress, makeup streaked with tears, hair tangled, heart frayed. Just as Rellik wanted me, I was sure, small, powerless, broken.

Does Vale know?

Was he still waiting for me so that we could head to the banquet? Did his men get to him?

He was expecting me. And I was gone.

No phone.

No way out.

And no idea what Rellik was going to say or do when he got here.

Valentino POV

I paced the room, glass of whiskey barely touched. My phone buzzed again. This time, it wasn't one of my lieutenants; it was Alejandro, one of the men I use for surveillance.

"We found her."

I stopped breathing.

"Where?"

"House on the edge of Falcon Heights. Gated. Not one of Rellik's usual spots, but we spotted the van and one of his men posted out front."

"Who?"

"Guy named John."

John.

The name hit like a punch to the gut. There was history there. Rellik's shadow. And worse, Victoria's driver. Loyal. Watchful. A spy in disguise.

"She's with her brother," I muttered.

"Looks that way."

A pause.

"You want us to hit it?"

I downed the whiskey and slammed the glass on the table. It burned going down, but I welcomed the fire. It grounded me. Kept me from putting a bullet in someone before we had a plan.

"She was waiting for our car when they took her," I growled, the words scraping out of me like gravel. "Gear up. We hit the house in twenty. I want her out."

The room snapped into motion. Chairs scraped back. Weapons were checked. No one asked questions.

But I knew the one on everyone's mind.

And Rellik?

I clenched my jaw, every muscle in my body coiled tight.

"That motherfucker's mine."

If he stood in my way, between Victoria and me, I'd put a bullet between his eyes even if it killed me.

VICTORIA POV

I pressed my ear to the door, fingers fidgeting with the silver clasp on my bracelet. I'd worn it tonight because I thought Vale would notice it. He always did before.

Stupid.

Stupid to believe I'd make it to him.

Stupid to think Rellik would ever let me be happy.

"John!" I called out, voice cracking. I knocked hard. "Please! You don't have to do this!"

Silence.

"I'm not a prisoner! I'm not some damn secret that needs to be locked away just because I crossed the street!"

Still nothing.

My voice cracked again. "Do you think Rellik will thank you for this? Do you think locking me up is protecting me? Because all you've done is make me hate him even more, and now I hate you too."

A beat of silence.

Then.

"Tori."

His voice. Muffled. Behind the door.

I ran to it. "John, please. Let me out. You know I wasn't doing anything wrong."

"Tori, you have to realize," he whispered. "It's not up to me."

"I wasn't being reckless. I was just, I was finally happy. For the first time in so long."

A pause. I pressed my forehead against the wood, breath shaky.

"You care about me, just like family," I whispered. "You always have. Please, John. Help me."

He didn't respond at first. I thought he might. I felt it.

But then.

Footsteps.

Walking away.

"John!" I slammed my fist against the door. "*Por favor*, I'm not a prisoner! I'm his sister!"

No answer.

I slid down the door, knees folding beneath me, hands over my face. The tears came hard this time, not just from fear, but from something worse.

What will Vale do when he finds out?

What if I don't see him again?

And that's when I saw it again. The image.

A flash, a distinct blur.

Right before the van sped through the red light.

Behind the palm trees.

There was something, no, someone watching. A figure. Half-shadowed. Still. Too still.

I didn't imagine it.

I'd turned my head just before the tires screamed, just before my shoulder slammed into the van wall. And I'd seen it.

A person.

Not moving, not running. Just watching.

The memory clawed its way back like a bruise surfacing under skin. Who were they? What were they waiting for?

And why the hell didn't they stop it?

I opened my eyes. The room was still and cold.

The shadows twisted on the wall again. And I swear, just for a second, I saw that silhouette again.

But when I blinked, it was gone.

The silence makes it worse. It's not just the four walls closing in; it's the memories, too. It's the way the cold air hits my skin and how the shadows in the room twist into something far too familiar.

I closed my eyes, trying to regulate my breathing. My heart. My mind.

But suddenly, I'm not there anymore.

I'm eighteen again.

The house smells like *arroz con pollo* and old leather. The windows are shut, but voices cut through the walls, tense, angry. My father's voice was loud and firm. And Rellik's sharper, younger, desperate to sound grown.

Papi left that day. And Rellik lost it.

I remember things breaking, glass, a chair, something ceramic. He was raging, throwing things. Hours passed.

Papi hadn't returned.

And then.

Bang.

A car crashed right into the driveway.

Hard.

I screamed or tried to. But Rellik was already there, grabbing me, dragging me down the hallway by the arm.

"No, wait, what was that?! Was that Papi?!" I screamed, fought, and clawed at his shirt.

But he didn't stop.

He shoved me into the closet.

Slammed it shut.

Locked it.

I pounded on the door, sobbing so hard I couldn't catch my breath.

"I need to know what's going on! Rellik!"

Nothing.

Just silence.

Just like now.

Tears sting my eyes. My throat tightens. I slide further down the wall, curling into myself, hands shaking, chest heaving like it might cave in.

I've been here before.

Locked away.

Shut out when I needed answers.

Trapped, when all I wanted was the truth.

"John," I whisper, voice hoarse. "I'm not a little girl anymore, I deserve to know what's going on."

Still nothing.

I wipe my face, though more tears slip through. I lean my head back, stare at the ceiling, wishing it would crack open and set me free.

But the only thing that caves in is me.

My eyes close again.

And I must've drifted off. But not for long.

It started with a low rumble.

Engines.

Multiple.

I scrambled to my feet, stumbling toward the window, but it was covered and blacked out from the outside with just a small hole that I could barely peek out of. I pressed my eye to it.

Just enough space to see a flash of headlights.

 Then I heard the first slam of metal on metal. Doors opening. Boots hitting the cement. Voices shouting.

Then...

Gunshots.

Everywhere.

Close.

Loud.

Each one cracking through the walls like thunder, like bones breaking right outside.

I dropped to the floor, hands clamped over my ears.

My breathing turned shallow, too fast. I couldn't get enough air. The room spun. My chest wouldn't rise. My lungs felt like they were caving in.

Were they here for me?

Were they here to kill?

Cartel?

The SUV from the plaza?

"John!" I screamed, my voice barely human. "John, what's happening?"

No answer.

Only more shots.

Then crash, something hit the roof above me. Heavy. Hard.

I curled tighter, trembling, teeth clenched. My fingertips went numb. My skin buzzed, like every nerve had turned to static. I crawled toward the bed, tried to wedge myself beneath it, but only half of me fit. The dress clung to my legs like plastic wrap. I gave up, dropping beside the bed between the post and the wall.

My back pressed into cold wood. My knees to my chest.

Boom.

Another shot. Closer now.

The wall shook.

My vision blurred. My hearing was muffled like I was underwater. Drowning in sound and silence all at once.

Was this it?

Was I going to die here?

Alone?

Trapped?

Another voice shouting commands. Rapid gunfire in response. A scream.

And still, I stayed curled on the floor, shaking. A part of me is still that terrified eighteen-year-old girl locked in the closet. Just waiting for the chaos to stop. I was waiting for someone to open the door and tell me it was over. Or worse, no one ever would

I could still smell the paint from that closet door, the sour sting of blood. I'd counted the scratches in the wood over and over, trying to distract myself from the sound of screaming downstairs, and that night blurred into every nightmare since.

I hated how fast I regressed. One moment, I was fighting to be strong, the next, I was ten steps behind, curling inward like I was still a scared girl no one came for.

I curled tighter, rocking now. Back and forth. It was my coping mechanism. My nails dug into my arms, red crescents rising in my skin. The air was thick, so thick it felt like I was choking.

And then...

His voice.

Muffled at first. Then louder, cutting through the chaos like a siren through fog.

"Victoria!"

God.

Vale.

"Vale*!*" I tried to scream, but it caught in my throat. A cracked whisper, strangled by tears. "I'm here*!*"

More footsteps. Shouting. Something shattered downstairs, glass, maybe? A table? The whole house trembled.

But I knew that voice.

I knew it like my own heartbeat.

"Victoria, answer me*!*"

He sounded furious. Desperate. Alive.

And that's when it hit me.

He came.

I crawled across the floor, dragging myself toward the door. My limbs felt like stone, but I didn't care. I pressed both palms flat against the wood and pounded with everything I had left.

"I'm here!" I screamed. "Valentino! I'm right here!"

Gunfire erupted again so close it shook the walls. I ducked, instinct taking over, hands over my head as I dropped flat to the floor, sobbing.

"*Vale,*" I whispered. "Please find me."

The last thing I heard was his voice, shouting my name again.

BOOM.

Something slammed against the house so hard it rattled the ceiling. My window shattered, shards raining across the floor, and I fell sideways with a cry.

The door creaked.

I scrambled to my knees, heart thundering so loud I couldn't hear anything else. Light spilled in from the hallway, golden, warm, like freedom.

"Vale?" I whispered, crawling forward, hands trembling as I reached out toward the light.

But when the door swung open fully.

It wasn't him.

A broad silhouette filled the frame. A gun slung across his chest. The hallway behind him was dim and hazy with dust.

One of Rellik's men.

I froze. That thin, fragile thread of hope I'd been clinging to for the last ten minutes snapped in half.

"No," I whispered, retreating. "Where is he? Where's Vale?"

He stepped forward.

"Get up," he barked, reaching for me.

I scrambled back, palms dragging against the floor, feet slipping.

"Don't touch me!"

Then.

A roar.

Not human.

Vale.

His footsteps thundered, a storm charging down the hall.

CRASH.

A blur of motion slammed into the man; Vale filled with rage. The two of them collided with bone-cracking force, crashing into the wall. Fists flew. A punch. Another. The sound of impact was sickening.

"Get the fuck away from her!" Vale bellowed.

I screamed as the two men tore through the hallway, the fight vicious, unrelenting. The walls shook with it.

I backed into the farthest corner, adrenaline crashing over me like a wave.

"Vale!" I cried again, louder this time, my voice breaking.

He turned.

Chest heaving. Knuckles bloodied. Eyes wild, then softening.

"Victoria."

He said it like a prayer.

And in that moment, I saw everything in his eyes.

The rage.

The fear.

The relief.

The love.

And then.

He was reaching for me.

CHAPTER 8

The moment his arms wrapped around me, the rest of the world vanished. Just for a second, no noise, no smoke. Just Vale and me.

Nothing else mattered.

 Until we weren't safe anymore.

Gunshots still cracked in the distance, muffled behind walls, echoing through the hall, but I barely registered them. All I could hear was the pounding of his heart beneath my ear, wild and frantic, mirroring my own.

"I thought I lost you," he whispered, voice hoarse, his hands framing my face like I might disappear again if he let go. "I thought they took you and I'd never…"

The words crumbled at the edge of his mouth, broken by the weight of the fear still clawing at him.

"You came," I choked out. All I could think about once they shoved me into the van, doors slamming behind me, was him. Even when I was tied up passing King Street, my thoughts were of Vale. But hearing his voice now? Seeing him here? I was unraveling all over again. "I didn't think you'd find me."

"I will always find you." His voice cracked. "I don't

care what side of the city they hide you in. I will tear, burn, dismantle every part of every city if I have to."

His hands trembled against my cheeks. My breath hitched. I could taste blood in my mouth; I hadn't even realized I'd bitten down that hard to stay quiet earlier.

A door slammed somewhere down the corridor.

His body stiffened. The moment shattered.

"We have to move," he said, the softness gone from his voice, replaced by something colder. Sharper.

King Vale had returned.

I clung to him, fingers fisting the fabric of his jacket. "It was Rellik," I gasped. "He knew about the event. He, he sent them before I could even get to the car."

His jaw clenched so hard I could hear his teeth grinding. "I swear to God, Victoria, I'll deal with him. But right now, we're getting you out."

I nodded, but my whole body trembled. "I couldn't breathe. They locked me in here like, like when…"

His expression shifted. Darkened. "Like the night your father died."

My heart stuttered.

He said it with such certainty. With weight.

But he wasn't there that night.

Was he?

That night had always been a blur of chaos and smoke. I could still sense the tears, blood, Rellik locking the door, followed by my screams, I can still hear in my sleep. I never thought Vale was anywhere near the house. But the way he said it, like he knew. Like he remembered.

Something cold and familiar trickled down my spine.

He pulled me back into him, tighter this time, like he could sense the flicker of doubt rising in my chest, or maybe he was trying to smother it before it grew teeth.

"No one locks you away from me ever again," he murmured. "Not even your brother."

His lips brushed my forehead, soft and searing. A promise inked into skin.

I drank in his scent, his cologne, smoke, sweat, gunmetal, and safety. It hit me all at once just how much I'd missed that scent. That steadiness.

Someone shouted outside. Another crack of gunfire.

He pulled back just enough to meet my eyes.

"We need to move," he said, low and urgent. "Can you walk?"

"With you?" I nodded. "Always."

Vale took my hand, and we moved fast.

The hallway was dim, and the air was still thick with smoke. Adrenaline buzzed in the air like static. Shouts echoed in the distance as Rellik's men scrambled, caught off guard by the ambush. I didn't look back. Didn't want to see John. Even if he was conflicted, he still let this happen. Whatever guilt he carried didn't matter now.

Vale, never let go of me. He wrapped his arm around me; head tucked in between it and his chest. His body moved like a shield, blocking me from any danger, every step forward a promise: *I'm not letting you go again.*

We reached the side exit.

I turned my head just a glance, instinct, and froze.

Headlights flared at the edge of the tree line.

One.

Two.

Then a third.

A black car pulled in, faster than the others. Aggressive. Familiar.

Too familiar.

My stomach dropped. My blood ran cold.

"Vale," I whispered, grabbing his arm.

He turned, following my gaze. I felt him tense beside me, every muscle locking into place.

Another door slammed.

And then I saw him.

Rellik.

He stepped out like a shadow, standing tall beside the car door. Six feet of silence, black shirt, black gloves, hair slicked back. His eyes were hidden behind dark sunglasses, even though night had already swallowed the sky. And still, I could feel his gaze on me.

The street light flickered overhead, catching just enough silver at his slightly tanned wrist to make it glint as he raised a hand and signaled his men.

Valentino moved instantly.

"Inside. Car. Now."

My legs finally responded, but my eyes wouldn't.

They stayed locked on him.

My brother was here.

He was probably already on his way before the ambush.

Coming over as soon as he had hung up with John.

I stumbled after Vale, heart pounding like war drums in my chest, each beat echoing run, but my mind kept screaming, look back.

Because no matter what he'd done, no matter how far he'd gone.

He was still Rellik.

Still, my brother.

And I remembered.

The night everything changed.

The way my hands shook around the doorknob that wouldn't turn.

The suffocating dark of the closet.

And then.

Light.

The door creaked open, and there he was.

Rellik.

Covered in blood.

Our father's blood.

Eyes wild. Breathing ragged.

He pulled me out and didn't say a word at first, just wrapped me in his arms and held on like the world might end if he let go.

Then he whispered,

"I'll always protect you, Tori. No matter what."

I didn't know why he had locked me in,
but I remember everything after he let me out.

I stumbled again, next to Vale.

Two of his men were already by the SUV, one bleeding from the arm, but still holding position like stone.

"Clear path going forward," one said with a nod. "Two minutes before, more show up."

Vale didn't hesitate. He yanked the back door open, pulled me in beside him, and barked, "*Vámonos. Drive.*"

I took one last look back.

As the door slammed shut behind me.

There he was.

My brother.

Rellik.

Just staring at me.

His expression was unreadable.

No emotion.

Stern.

Solid.

Almost like a statue.

If he had any emotion, he was holding it in, just like a storm waiting to land.

The engine roared. Gunshots rang out behind us, but we were already speeding through the darkness.

I held up my right hand and placed it onto my chest, trying to steady my breathing. Everything was happening too fast. And somehow, not fast enough.

I didn't feel safe.

Not yet.

Not until we were miles away.

Not until I knew Rellik couldn't find me again.

Vale didn't speak at first. He just watched me, his eyes tracing every inch of my face like he was still trying to believe I was really here.

"You, okay?" he asked finally, voice low and raw.

I nodded, even though I wasn't sure if it was true. "Where are we going?"

"My beach house," he said. "No one knows about it except my most trusted men. It's the only place I can think of where he can't reach you."

Beach house?

I tried to picture it, but couldn't.

All I could focus on was the warmth of his hand still wrapped around mine. The image of the city lights behind us, the sound of tires burning rubber as we head toward our freedom.

I turned toward the window, and there it was.

A sign that I needed.

A sign to show hope

A sign to feel free.

Just ahead of us, glowing in the dark.

With big, bold letters.

Now Leaving Gravenport.

We were officially out of the city.

I let out a breath I hadn't even realized I'd been holding.

Valentino glanced over, like he'd felt the shift in me.

"Talk to me."

"I saw King Street when they were taking me," I whispered. "I was so close to where you were. But they turned before I could scream."

A pause.

"I thought I was going to disappear forever."

His jaw tightened. "You were right there," he said bitterly. "And I wasn't fast enough."

"Yes, you were," I said, reaching for him. "You came. You didn't have to, but you came for me."

He looked away, eyes glassy for a moment. "I can't lose you again, Victoria. I already..."

He stopped.

Jaw flexing.

Staring straight ahead.

Already what?

But I didn't ask.

Not yet.

I leaned my head against his shoulder, letting the rhythm of the road calm the ache in my chest. My body was still raw with fear, but here in this car, with him, it felt like I could finally exhale. I closed my eyes and rested.

We drove deeper into the night.

Toward the crashing waves.

Toward the promise of quiet and safety.

The tires crunched over gravel as we turned onto a secluded driveway lined with tall palm trees and deeper shadows. I could hear the ocean now, just past the dunes, steady, crashing, untamed.

It was the first thing that felt real in hours.

Vale glanced at me as the SUV slowed to a stop.

"We're here," he said gently.

I nodded; my hand still locked in his.

Eyes slowly opening.

My whole body still buzzed with adrenaline and confusion, but I managed to open the door and step out.

The breeze hit me salty, cold, alive.

The sunrise just beyond the horizon.

The house was quiet.

Modern.

Tucked just far enough from the world to feel like a secret.

Safe.

Vale double-checked every lock, every window, every blind like a man expecting the world to break in at any second.

But when he turned to face me again, something in his eyes shifted.

Softened.

The kind of softness he never showed anyone else.

The kind he reserved only for me.

"You're safe here," he said quietly. "I promise."

I nodded, though my voice was lost somewhere between exhaustion and the tidal wave of emotion crashing behind my ribs.

I stood there in the middle of the beach house living room, arms crossed over my chest, the silence between us thick, still so much lingering in the air.

As the adrenaline began to fade, I took in the details of the space that somehow already smelled like safety.

There were photos on the mantle of Vale and his mother, younger, smiling. A time I'd never known. I didn't ask about them. Didn't dare touch. I just let my eyes wander.

The walls were painted a soft blue, trimmed in crisp white. My bare feet sank into the thick rug by the couch, grounding me.

I stared at the floor for a long time, until I found the courage to look at him again.

When I did, he was already moving toward me.

Vale crossed the space between us and reached into the inner pocket of his jacket.

"I was going to give you this last night, after the banquet," he said, his voice low and uneven. "But after everything that just happened, I need you to have this now."

He pulled out a small, dark velvet box.

Something fluttered inside me, unexpected and profound.

Inside was a silver necklace, delicate but strong. The chain was open, one end a tail, the other end shimmered in the low light, a small, open silver heart. Not decorative. When you put the two ends together, it creates a lock.

The kind that required just the right twist of the tail to secure the heart.

Vale stepped closer and gently placed it into my hand.

"It only opens for the person who knows the right way to twist it," he said. "Like us, I guess."

My fingers traced the shape. I still couldn't speak.

Then, quietly, he reached into his pocket and pulled out a second, smaller box.

When I opened it, I gasped.

Nestled inside was a slim silver ring. Elegant. Timeless.

But it wasn't the design that made my eyes glare with happiness.

It was what was inside the ring.

Under a delicate dome of clear resin, frozen in time, was a tiny larkspur flower.

The same flower that Vale wore inside his pendant.

The same one Rellik and I once left at my father's grave.

The same one that had once meant everything.

"I had it made a long time ago," he said, voice barely above a whisper. "Back when I didn't know if I'd ever see you again. It was always meant to be yours."

My throat tightened. "Why now?"

His eyes found mine, full of something raw. Unfiltered.

"Because no matter how much I try to keep you at a distance…"

He exhaled, shaking his head.

"I can't. You're not just part of my past, Victoria. You're my only future."

The way he said my name made my heart throb.

I slid the ring onto my finger. It fit perfectly.

It seemed like it had been waiting for me, too.

And when he reached up to clasp the necklace around my neck, I noticed the way his hands trembled.

The lock clicked into place.

And for just a moment, something in me finally settled.

Like maybe this stolen moment on the edge of war was ours to keep.

He stood so close now that I could feel his breath on my skin.

The necklace was still cold against my chest, the silver heart resting just below my collarbone.

And just like that, something in me cracked wide open.

All the fear.

All the running.

All the pretending I was fine without him.

None of it mattered anymore.

Not here.

Not now.

Not after what we'd just survived.

I didn't care that we'd been torn apart.

Didn't care that the world outside hated what we were together.

In this moment, all I wanted was him.

"Valentino," I whispered, voice barely there. "Take me."

His mouth crashed into mine before the words had even entirely left.

He tasted like adrenaline and hunger and all the things I'd been craving in silence.

There was no hesitation.

He didn't take the time to unravel any part of me.

Just raw, desperate need.

His hands were everywhere. My jaw, my waist, my hips. He lifted me like I weighed nothing and placed me gently on the edge of the kitchen counter.

"I want you," he whispered into my ear. "Every inch of you."

I leaned into every touch, every graze of his hands like they were the only thing keeping me from falling apart.

My legs wrapped around him, pulling him closer, deeper like I wanted to fuse myself to him.

My fingers tangled in his hair, and I tilted my head back as his mouth moved up from between my thighs and then found the edge of my collarbone.

And then.

He did something unexpected.

His fingers found the heart at the base of my neck, the silver one he'd just given me, and tugged the tail, gently at first.

The necklace tightened. Just slightly.

Rising higher on my throat.

I gasped.

Not from fear.

From something completely opposite

Arousal.

The pressure was subtle. Perfectly controlled.

But it made my skin buzz.

Made my breath catch.

He paused, watching me.

"Too much?"

"No," I confessed quietly, voice shaky. "Don't stop."

The heart now rested against the hollow of my throat, like it belonged there.

Like he belonged there.

It was possessive, but careful.

Powerful but tender.

He kissed the spot where silver met skin, his lips slowly moving up and down, inch by inch, deliberately. Reverent.

"You're mine," he growled, voice rough with emotion.

"Every part of you. Every scar. Every secret. Every breath."

And in that moment, I gave myself to him completely. I released.

Mind.

Body.

Soul.

I let him see everything.

The pieces that were broken.

The parts I didn't show anyone else.

And as he held me tighter, carrying me to the living room, like he already knew every inch, I realized I wasn't afraid of being claimed anymore.

Because I had never really stopped being his.

His arms wrapped around me; our legs intertwined beneath a blanket. We were now on the oversized rug in the beach house living room, finishing up round two.

Outside, the waves whispered softly against the shore, and for once, for a rare, perfect moment, everything was still.

Hours passed as we just held each other. Not wanting to let go.

My heart was beating for entirely different reasons.

I was calm.

I felt safe.

Vale was my anchor.

Just like he was when I was eighteen.

And he still is, six years later.

The fire we'd lit earlier that day had dimmed to glowing embers, casting flickers of gold and orange across his bare chest.

I lay my head against him, fingers tracing the line of his tattoo, crowning his heart.

The same chest I used to fall asleep on when we were just kids pretending we weren't about to risk it all.

His hand moved slowly through my hair, soothing and steady, like he was memorizing the weight of me all over again.

"You always do that when you're overthinking," he murmured, eyes half-closed.

"Do what?"

"Draw shapes on me," he said softly. "You used to do stars, now it's crowns."

I didn't answer at first.

I was too wrapped up in the way he knew me.

Too lost in the fact that, even after everything, he still remembered things I didn't know I was still doing.

"I'm just thinking," I finally said.

"About?"

I hesitated, then sat up slightly, resting my hand flat over his chest.

"Earlier, when you said that comment. About the night my father died."

His body tensed just a flicker, something unspoken stirring beneath the surface.

He didn't look away, but he stopped stroking my hair.

"I thought you weren't there that night," I whispered.

"Vale, were you?"

He didn't answer right away.

The silence between us cracked open like a fault line.

"I..."

BANG. BANG. BANG.

A harsh knock shattered the moment, echoing against the front door like a warning.

Not a polite knock. Not a "neighborly" knock.

A message.

How did we not hear the car pull up?

Were we so lost in time that everything else ceased to matter?

Was it Rellik? Had he found us?

No.

He wouldn't knock.

He'd break the door down.

I froze, instinctively clutching the blanket tighter around me.

Vale was already on his feet, pants half-buttoned, grabbing the gun tucked inside a drawer near the door.

My heart thudded so loudly I swore they could hear it from the other side.

"Stay here," he said sharply, voice shifting cold, precise, lethal.

"Vale."

"*Quédate.*"

Another round of knocks, louder now.

Then silence.

It was over.

The quiet was gone.

And whatever peace we'd built in that room, whatever truth was starting to rise had vanished into the crashing surf behind us.

The heavy knocking was replaced by murmurs just outside the door, hushed voices laced with urgency.

Vale glanced through the peephole, then turned back toward me.

"It's my guys, my firsts," he said, voice tight.

I was already out of the blanket, searching for my dress.

Vale signaled me to the bedroom.

I didn't ask questions. Didn't move toward him like I wanted.

I didn't want to ruin the moment we'd been having.

I slipped into the bedroom to finish dressing.

By the time I stepped back out in one of Vale's black button-downs that luckily completely covered me, he was closing the door behind the men responsible for the knocks.

Two men stood there.

I recognized one Luca, tall, scarred, razor-sharp jaw, and a stare that made people rethink their life choices.

The other was younger. Latino, sharp eyes, thick gold chain around his neck.

They both stopped when they saw me.

Questions flickered in their eyes, quick, but quiet.

They looked away, not wanting to upset their King.

Vale shot them a rugged look that said, "Respect your Queen."

Then each of them gave me a nod.

"What's going on?" I asked, wrapping my arms around myself.

Luca spoke first, low and controlled, waiting for Vale's approval to continue.

"Boss, we've got a problem. Word's coming in from *La Corona* and it's bad."

Vale didn't move. "How bad?"

The younger one stepped forward. "Rellik's gang, the Killers, they're hitting South Side fronts. One by one. Fast."

"They've already wrecked Crown Spirits on 9th, Crown Side Auto on Regal, and someone set fire to the back lot of Charlotte's."

Vale's face didn't change, but I saw the rage rising

from his spine like smoke.

"Any casualties?" he asked.

"Not yet," Luca said, "but it's not just damage. It's a message."

They all looked at me. Quietly. Just for a second.

My stomach dropped.

"This is about me," I whispered. "Isn't it?"

No one answered. They didn't need to.

Valentino stepped closer, cupping the side of my face with a gentleness that contradicted the storm in his eyes.

"This isn't your fault, Victoria."

But I could see it all clicking together. The heat, the retaliation, the lines being drawn in every direction.

I had broken the one rule, never cross into the South Side, and now the consequences were coming for both of us.

I wanted to hate Rellik for what he'd done. But he was still my brother. The one who'd held me close when I was broken. The one who'd promised to keep me safe even if that promise came with chains I couldn't escape. How had love turned into this war?

"He's not going to stop," I said, my breath shaky. "Not until he gets what he wants. His sister, back home."

"He's not taking you anywhere," Vale growled, voice low and final.

I looked at the men again, and for the first time, I saw the beginning of war in their silence.

Were these men really going to die for their new Queen?

A Queen who never asked for this, who just wanted to be with the man she loved.

Just then, Luca's phone buzzed. He answered, stepping a few feet away, though I could still hear the clipped urgency in his voice.

He returned, jaw clenched. "We just got word. One of ours, Tony from Gallows Park, was jumped. He's alive, barely. They dumped him near Dead Mile, with a broken jaw and a message carved into his chest."

My stomach turned. "What kind of message?"

Luca looked at Vale. "Midnight—the docks. Fight or fall.

The room fell silent.

A direct challenge.

Is my brother fucking serious?

What is this, eighth grade?

I watched Vale, and for the first time, I saw something in his eyes that scared me, not just anger.

Resolve.

Vengeance.

"The Killers want war," the younger soldier muttered.

"No," Vale said, voice cutting through me like steel. "Their Leader does. If Rellik wants war, that's what he'll get." He turned to me, stepping closer, hand tightening around mine.

"I won't let him destroy what we're trying to build. I won't lose you again."

His thumb brushed my cheek gently, grounding me and yet somehow setting everything inside me on fire.

I wanted to believe him, I tried to think we could come out of this ash with something good, something solid. But fear whispered the truth. Every moment with him was a stolen one, fragile and impossible to hold forever. Rellik will make sure of that.

Midnight was more than a time of day. It was something that Gravenport would talk about for decades. A true reckoning. A point of no return. And this time, it wouldn't be about whispers and warnings.

It would be blood.

CHAPTER 9

The room cleared out fast after the call, but Vale didn't follow. Not right away.

He stood on the porch of the beach house, facing the dark horizon the sunset had brought in, his back to me. The wind tangled through his shirt, and moonlight shimmered across the surface of the waves below. His fists clenched tightly around the railing of the wraparound deck. I didn't have to see his face; I felt it in the air around him. He was already picturing the fight.

I stepped outside, barefoot on the cool wood, and walked toward him. The night was heavy, like it knew what was coming.

I wrapped my hands around his face and pressed my forehead to his, forcing him to meet me. I had to stand on tiptoe to reach his eyes, but I didn't care. He turned away, not wanting to face me.

My heart was a war zone of its own, caught between the man who always protected me and the man who would burn the whole city down for me.

Maybe that's why I always chose Valentino, the so-called villain. Because he would sacrifice the world to save me. Even if it meant going through my brother to do it.

I stepped closer, my voice low, fragile.

"Vale, don't do this."

He didn't turn around.

"I have to."

"No," I said, louder this time. Firmer. "You want to. You want this war."

He spun toward me then, eyes sharp, jaw tight, mouth set in that dangerous line I knew too well.

"He hit you, Victoria. He took you. Locked you up like some piece of property." His voice cracked. "I let my guard down for one second, and he got to you."

I reached for his hand and pressed it to my chest. "But I'm here. You found me. You brought me back."

His jaw twitched, eyes flicking between mine.

"Because I stormed the fucking gates to get to you. If I don't answer this, he'll think he can do it again. Or worse. And next time..."

"There can't be a next time," I cut in, heart pounding. "Vale, please. I know Rellik. He's coming undone. He's not thinking clearly."

"There's something between you that neither of you guys has resolved." I snapped.

Vale's laugh was bitter and hollow. "And I'm supposed to just what, sit and watch while he tears through my side of the city?"

"No," I whispered. "But maybe there's a way out of this that doesn't end with one of you buried in Gravenport cemetery.

My stomach twisted. "How the hell did we even end up like this?"

He exhaled sharply. His breath hitched, and something behind his eyes shattered.

"And do what you need to stay alive," I begged. "I can't survive that, not if I lose either one of you. Not again. Not after everything."

His gaze searched mine, raw and unsure. "You want me to fight and somehow not win?"

"I want you both to survive," I said. "That's what I want. I want a miracle. A fucking Hail Mary."

He ran a hand over his face like he was trying to rub the war out of his skin. Then he reached for me, fingers slipping around the back of my neck.

"You're asking me to spare the man who tried to break us, again."

"I'm asking you to remember the boy you once called your brother," I said softly. "Because deep down, I think he still remembers you, too. You wouldn't still wear that necklace if you didn't believe it mattered."

His fingers brushed the chain at his throat. Then held steady at the pendent. He glanced at the Larkspur Flower as if a memory was replaying in his head.

"Just think about it," I whispered. "Maybe it's not

enough to stop this. But maybe it's enough not to destroy each other. Not completely."

He looked away. "There's no talking to a man like Rellik anymore. You saw him. He's gone. He's made up his mind, like you said, he's coming undone."

"Then be different," I said. "Choose something else."

He turned back to me, eyes blazing. "I already did."

My breath caught. "What does that mean?"

"It means I chose you. And because of that, there's no walking away from this. I either end this tonight or I lose everything. I lose you."

My heart dropped.

I grabbed his shirt, pulled him closer to me, and looked straight into his eyes. My voice cracked as I said, "If you fight him, if you kill him, I don't know what that'll do to me. After everything, *Todavía es mi hermano*. After Papi, he's all I have."

He froze, like those words had shattered something in him.

Then slowly, deliberately he cupped my face in both hands, holding me like I might slip through his fingers.

"I'm not letting anyone hurt you again," he said. "You have me now."

The silence stretched long and cruel. Somewhere, a clock ticked past nine. Midnight was not far.

I rested my forehead against his, tears threatening. "Then promise me one thing."

"Anything."

"If there's a moment, any moment, where you can choose not to pull that trigger, promise me, you'll take it. For me."

He swallowed hard. His voice was almost too soft. "I... I promise."

But I heard it. The break in his voice. The part of him that already knew how this night would end.

He pulled away slowly, fingers brushing mine. His eyes lingered, memorizing me.

As if he wasn't sure he'd ever get the chance again.

"I have to go," he said.

"Don't," I choked out. "Just stay. Please."

But he didn't.

He kissed me instead. Slow and deep, no goodbye, no promise. Just the fire between us, and the tether we'd always had.

And then he was gone.

I stayed on the porch for a few moments longer after he left, staring at the spot where his car had disappeared into the night. Then I turned around and stepped back inside.

The door clicked shut behind me. The beach house

felt too quiet. Too hollow. It was like it had been drained of oxygen. I was suffocating.

I stood there, frozen in the silence, waiting for clarity to come rushing in. But it didn't.

All I could hear was the rush of my heartbeat. All I could feel was the pain.

I had just begged him to spare my brother, but I knew Vale. I knew that look in his eyes.

If Rellik raised a weapon, he would raise hell.

And if it came down to it, only one of them would survive.

I sat down on the edge of the bed, trying to breathe, trying to stop shaking. But I couldn't.

Not when I realized something awful.

Maybe I was the only one who could stop this.

I shoved my feet into my shoes with trembling fingers. There was no time for logic. No time for plans.

I didn't know if this was the biggest mistake of my life or the bravest thing I'd ever do, but I knew where I had to go.

To him.

To Rellik.

If there was even a sliver of space left between the two men I loved, maybe I was the only one who could fill it before the fire consumed everything.

I got in the car and gave the order to drive. They didn't question it, maybe out of loyalty, or maybe because no one wanted to challenge the girl Vale had just promised to burn the city down for.

But that was the least of my worries. Time was against me at this point.

Every streetlight we passed felt like a ticking clock. Every shadow was a reminder that I was either too late or dangerously close to just in time.

My hands were gripping the door handle so tightly that I could barely feel my fingers. My thoughts wouldn't stop.

What am I doing?

This is insane. This is reckless.

Vale would kill me if he knew I'd left the beach house. He was fighting to keep me safe, and here I was driving straight into the middle of a war.

But it was the only thing that made sense.

I couldn't let them kill each other.

I couldn't live in a world where one of them didn't exist.

Or both.

Oh God.

What if I lost them both?

My breath caught in my throat. I started to panic, shaking my head, trying to force the thought away.

Pull yourself together, Tori. C'mon.

Vale was the man who knew my soul, who called me Victoria when the world only ever saw Tori. Who touched me like I was sacred? Who kissed me like I was something he needed to believe in.

But Rellik.

Rellik was blood.

Family.

The boy who learned to tie my shoes and braid my hair after Mami died. Who protected me from the worst of the world, even as he slowly became a part of it?

He was my brother. My original anchor.

How was I supposed to choose between them?

How could I survive losing either one?

Tears blurred my vision as we rolled to a stoplight. I narrowed my eyes, blinking once, just in time to catch the sign: **The Marcanova Estate.**

My chest tightened. Just past this light, I would arrive.

I didn't know if he'd still be there.

But I had to try.

We slowed down, subtle enough not to draw

attention. My heart slammed against my ribs like it wanted out.

Please don't let me be too late. Please don't let him be gone already.

A phone buzzed from the back seat over and over. I didn't look. Couldn't.

Because I knew it was Vale since my phone was still in the street somewhere, this was obviously one he left behind on purpose.

This was it.

All I had was this moment, this gamble.

I wasn't sure if Rellik would even let me in.

I wasn't sure what I'd find when I got there.

But I had to make him listen.

He had to hear me before all of this turned to blood.

I took a breath as I turned the last corner, headlights washing over the towering black gates I thought I'd never lay eyes on again.

They were already open.

That should've been a warning.

The driveway was flooded with black motorcycles and matte SUVs, some still rumbling, their riders prowling nearby like wolves on standby. Leather cuts, tattoos, and cold eyes tracked me the second I stepped out of the car.

The Killers were here.

I had never seen so many at one time.

Every single one of them. Some from Papi's reign, others who came under Rellik.

And they weren't just here; they were waiting for blood. Thirsty for it.

One of them stepped toward me, face hidden under a bandana, gun on his hip. I froze, heart racing.

"You're not supposed to be here."

"Back off."

The voice that cut through the air didn't shout, but it had weight, a command sharpened by familiarity.

I turned, and there he was, John. He was alive.

Still wearing the same jacket from earlier, jaw tight and eyes swimming with conflict. I couldn't read John thoroughly, but I saw enough. He was angry but not towards me.

"Go inside," he told one of the others, who gave a half-scowl before obeying. Then his attention shifted to me.

"He's right, though. You shouldn't be here, Tori."

"I didn't come to be told where I should or shouldn't be," I snapped, voice trembling. "Where's my brother?"

John hesitated, then glanced around. "Come on."

Without another word, he guided me toward the back entrance. Past a row of stone columns. Past the silence that hung between us like a loaded gun.

He didn't touch me, but he walked close, close enough that it felt like a quiet apology.

When we reached the private hallway near the kitchen, he finally spoke again, low and gruff. "He's not going to approve you being here."

"Well," I exhaled, steadying my breath, "I'm not here for his approval. I'm here to stop him."

John gave me a look. "He's been off the rails since you disappeared. I've never seen him this way. It's almost like the night..."

He stopped himself. But I knew what he was going to say.

The night my dad died.

I think that's when he got the scar. That's why he never spoke about it, because it would bring back that awful night.

"You'd better know what you're doing."

I looked up at the closed door at the end of the hallway, the meeting room.

"I don't," I admitted. "But I'm still walking in."

John didn't stop me.

I didn't knock. I just pushed the door open.

Rellik stood with his back to me, shoulders hunched as he leaned over a table strewn with blueprints, maps, and grainy surveillance shots. Guns lined the wall behind him like art. The silence thickened the second I entered.

"I told them I didn't want anyone in here," he said without turning.

"That never applied to me," I whispered.

He froze. Tensed. Then it looked like he took a breath of relief.

And then he turned.

There it was, his face, the storm behind his hazel eyes. The muscle was ticking in his jaw like a clock counting down to violence.

I took a step forward. "Rellik..."

"No." He raised a hand, voice low but sharp. "You don't get to show up now, Tori."

"You had me taken!" I snapped, emotion choking the back of my throat. "Like I was property, like I was a threat. You locked me up!"

He said nothing.

"I was safe. I was going to be with someone who makes me feel like I exist again. And you took that. Why?"

"I didn't know where they were taking you, for sure," he muttered, avoiding my eyes. "I just gave the order."

"You mean you gave the order to stop me from living?" My voice cracked. "To stop me from choosing someone who isn't you."

Rellik flinched. Just barely.

"Please," I whispered, stepping closer. "I'm not here to fight. I came here to beg."

He still didn't speak, but he didn't move, either.

"I know what tonight means. I know what you're about to do. But you can't. This isn't just about territory anymore; it's personal. Too personal. You go through with this, and there's no turning back. Not for you. Not for him. Not for me."

"Tori…"

I interrupted him.

"Do you remember when I was eight, and I broke my ankle falling off that swing that Papi put up in the backyard?" My voice trembled. "You ran to the hospital. Papi told you to go home, but you stayed all night anyway. You didn't even leave to eat."

His jaw clenched.

"And when Mami died," I pressed on, words falling faster, more desperate. "I cried for what felt like forever, and you slept on the floor next to my bed every night so I wouldn't feel alone?"

His mouth stayed tight, unreadable.

"I'm still that girl, Rellik, your baby sister. Please don't make me lose you. Don't make me lose both of you.”

When he finally spoke, his voice was low. Steady.

“You won’t lose me.”

“But I will!” I cried. “If you kill each other, if you burn the South Side to the ground just to prove a point, what do I have left then?”

He turned back toward the table, grabbing a pistol and checking the chamber like my words were nothing but wind.

“I’m not letting Tino win, Tori. Not after what he’s taken.”

I was too emotional to comprehend what he meant by that. What had he taken? Was he referring to me?

“And what about what you’ve taken?” I whispered.

He froze. The air between us went still, pulsing with everything unspoken.

“I love him,” I said, soft but sharp as a blade. “And I love you. And it’s breaking me in half. But I can’t stand by while you turn this into a war that neither of you will walk away from.”

Slowly, he turned to face me again. “It’s too late.”

“No. No, it’s not.”

“It is,” he said again, final, hollow. “You should go, Tori. You came to try. You tried. But this ends tonight on the street as it should have years ago.”

The words crushed me.

So, I did the only thing I hadn't done in years.

I walked up and wrapped my arms around him, sobbing into his chest. He didn't move at first, but then his hand landed gently on my back.

"I'm sorry, baby sis," he murmured. "For everything. I should've never hit you. That'll be my biggest regret."

Then he pulled back just enough to say the rest. "But this, this is war."

And I knew then that was his goodbye. His, I love you.

Just like Vale.

There was no stopping it.

I sat there in silence, the weight of both their choices crushing me. My hands gripped the arms of the chair so tightly that I hadn't realized my knuckles had gone pale. I felt like a ghost barely breathing, just existing.

Everything inside me screamed to do something, to stop it, to shout louder or beg harder. But Rellik was immovable, and so was Vale. Two forces of nature headed for a collision I couldn't stop.

My brother was the storm.

Vale, the wildfire.

And I, I was the trembling ground beneath it all.

A sharp breath left me, and I pushed myself up from the chair. My knees nearly buckled. I didn't even know where I was going, only that I couldn't sit here and drown in this helplessness anymore. Maybe I'd walk forever. Perhaps I'd disappear.

Just as I reached the door, it creaked open.

John stood there, framed by the dim hallway light. His face softened when he saw me, and he gave a slight nod as if to say he knew. That made it worse.

"Going somewhere?" he asked gently, eyes scanning my face.

"I can't do this, John." My voice was raw, cracked. "I can't just sit here while they kill each other."

He stepped inside, closing the door behind him. "I know. That's why I stayed back. He figured you might need someone."

His words hit me like a ton of bricks. I didn't realize I was crying until I felt the tear fall to my lip. I turned away, embarrassed.

"Rellik told me to stay with you," he added after a pause. "Keep you updated. Give you the play-by-play. Again, this is to keep you updated, not to keep you here."

I froze. Then slowly, I turned to face John.

Rellik is not trying to keep me here, which means he feels like he has the advantage. I was conflicted. I turn to John, a little puzzled.

"Like a sport?" My voice was sharper than I meant it

to be, but I couldn't help it.

John didn't flinch. "No, like someone who knows you'd tear yourself apart if you were kept in the dark."

I wiped my face with the back of my hand and gave a slight nod.

"Okay," I whispered. "Then tell me everything."

He pulled out his phone and opened a live line.

"I am connected to another one of my guys who is there; he will tell me what's going on, and he's sending me a live feed, "John explained.

 I could already hear the background noise, shouts, engines rumbling, and the static tension of war.

"They're about to start moving in," he said quietly, eyes locked on the screen. "South Pier."

I sat back down. My knees gave out more easily this time. My hands were still trembling, and John noticed. He pulled a chair beside mine and sat close, but not too close. Anchoring me without overwhelming me.

All I could do now was listen.

And pray.

John held the phone between us, the screen casting a bluish glow in the dim room. His jaw was tight, knuckles whitening as he gripped the device like a lifeline. Every so often, his eyes flicked toward me, searching for a sign I could offer hope, though I had none to give. The signal buzzed for a second before connecting.

"They're moving," a voice said on the other end, breathless and low. "Approaching South Pier now, looks like our crew is splitting into two flanks. Tino's men are already stationed."

I sat frozen, every word sinking into my bones like ice water. My heartbeat hammered in my ears, drowning out everything else. The faint scent of salt hung in the air from the nearby shore, mingling with the room's staleness. My palms were clammy with sweat despite the chill, fingers trembling as they clenched the armrest.

"What about Valentino?" I asked, my voice barely above a whisper.

John held up a hand, eyes narrowing. "Hold on."

There was a pause, muffled shouting in the background, then the voice came back, more frantic.

"Shots fired! The north entrance lit up first. Kings came in fast. One of ours is down, I... shit, I think it was Eli."

My hands flew to my mouth, stifling a scream.

John's jaw clenched. "Do you see either one?"

"Negative. We've lost visual on both. Smokes everywhere. Someone set off a flash bomb, can't tell who. It's chaos. I think Tino's trying to flank, but wait, hold..."

Static.

"No, no, no," I breathed, leaning closer. "What's happening?"

John cursed and redialed. "Come on. Come on."

The line clicked back in.

"Update," John barked.

"We've got at least three of ours down. One of Tino's lieutenants took a hit, Luca, I think. Not sure how bad. Still no eyes on Rellik. Someone thought they saw him near the back dock, but…"

Another blast.

"Shit! Tino's there! He's going through our men like nothing!"

My blood ran cold. "What does that mean? Going through?"

"Gunfire everywhere, we're pushing hard. But the Kings are pushing back."

The line crackled again.

I gripped John's arm, fingers digging in. "What about my brother? Did they see him?"

"Still unclear," the voice replied, more rushed now. "Someone swore they saw him go down. Others think it may have been a decoy. It's mayhem out there."

I couldn't breathe.

"I can't lose both of them," I whispered, barely

audible.

John's hand landed steadily on my shoulder. "We'll know more soon. Just hold on."

But I couldn't hold on. Not really.

All I could do was sit there, drowning in every second that passed with death circling two of the men I loved most in this world, and there was no way to stop it.

John's grip on the phone tightened once more, knuckles white. The voice on the other end came back, strained and urgent.

"Wait. Wait, hold," heavy breathing, someone running, "they're stopping. The Killers and Kings, they're backing off. I think it's just the two of them now. They're facing off, Rellik and Tino. Just them."

I stood from the chair, knees trembling, and moved toward John, like being closer might somehow let me hear better.

"Describe it," I whispered. "Please."

"Crowd's circling them, but no one's stepping in. It's like they planned this. To go head-to-head. Rellik's got a blade drawn. Tino's not armed, at least not visibly."

John stared at the phone, as if his eyes alone could force better clarity through the speaker. I started pacing the room, my breath catching with every word.

"They're talking," the voice said. "Hold on. Let me

get closer."

Rustling.

"...used to be brothers," someone said on the other end. The voice wasn't clear, but the weight of it was.

The words hit like a hammer. I was suddenly back in our childhood backyard, where Rellik and Tino had laughed over scraped knees and sun-warmed afternoons. Back when the world was smaller, and nothing, nothing had shattered the bond between them.

My breath hitched.

Another voice answered, lower. Sharper. "You were my family."

Silence.

Then.

"You made me choose," the first voice said again. Tino, I think.

Followed by the other voice, which was cold and bitter.

 "You left me no choice, and you made me a liar," came Rellik's growl.

"They don't know the whole story, do they?" Tino shot back. "Because if they did, you wouldn't still be their Leader."

A pause. The background fell eerily quiet.

No gunfire. No movement.

Then, out of nowhere, a single gunshot.

Followed by shouting. A crack of glass.

And the line went dead.

"No!" I screamed.

John fumbled to reconnect. "Come on, damn it, come on."

Nothing.

Only the pulsing silence of the room.

And the terror closing in.

CHAPTER 10

The silence was unbearable.

I was silently going mad just thinking of all the different outcomes.

I stood there, frozen in place, staring at the dead phone in John's hand. My ears rang; my breath caught between a scream and a sob. That gunshot echoed louder in my head than anything else I'd ever heard. It drowned out reason. It drowned out hope. Was that the gunshot that changed my life forever?

John's lips were moving. I knew he was saying something, maybe trying to calm me down or make sense of what had just happened. But I couldn't hear him. All I could hear was that final moment, the words, the betrayal, the defining end.

Someone had been shot.

Someone I loved.

And I didn't know who.

I start to remember.

When Vale walked away, he had his gun tucked just inside his belt. And Rellik was double-checking his right before he told me goodbye. It could've been either one of them. This was torture. I needed answers.

The room tilted slightly as I stumbled back, clutching the edge of the chair for support. My chest felt like it was caving in, like my ribs had become a cage too tight for my lungs. Slowly closing in until I suffocate.

"John," I finally managed, my voice barely above a whisper. "I need answers. I need to be there, if one of them is dying as we speak, I need to be by their side," I sobbed.

He hesitated. "Tori, it's chaos out there. I don't even know where they are now. Communications are down. We lost all contact after that shot."

I shook my head. "No. Someone has to know something, one of your people, one of Vale's, someone. There's always someone watching, maybe I can ...."

"They will tell me," John replied with hesitation in his voice.

"They can't die; they can't. I NEED TO BE THERE," I said with panic still layering my vocals.

He didn't argue, but his silence spoke volumes.

 He was just as scared as I was.

He had been by Rellik's side for as long as I can remember. He was even under my father at one time.

He lost one leader. Was he ready to lose another?

I paced, dragging my fingers through my hair. Every second that ticked by felt like a lifetime, a lifetime of me not knowing who I lost. I kept seeing flashes of Rellik's eyes when he said it was too late to stop it, Vale's voice when he promised me I was his Queen.

Two men. Two hearts. And I was the breaking point between them.

God, please. Please let them both be okay.

I stopped pacing and turned to John. "If you get any update, even a whisper, even a rumor, you tell me. You hear me? I don't care if it's bad news. I need to know, please, you owe me."

Referring to being kidnapped and locked away while he did nothing.

He nodded. "I'll find out."

As he stepped out to make calls and hunt down answers, I sat in that same chair again. This time, not in defeat, but in prayer. In desperation. In hope.

Because I wasn't ready to lose either of them.

I understood now. As much as I wanted to be with Vale, I need Rellik in my life. These men complete me. Without either one, I would be broken forever.

I quickly ran to my old room, where Rellik always had a set of clothes for me. I needed to get out of this dress. It was ruined and a constant reminder of the other night. I changed into a t-shirt and leggings.

I moved to the window, unable to stay still. The glass was cold against my fingertips as I leaned into it, eyes scanning the quiet darkness beyond the trees. Nothing. Not a car. Not a sound. You would think some of them would have come back by now.

But then I saw him.

A figure barely visible standing near the edge of the property line, not moving. Not smoking. Not talking, just standing there.

My heart skipped. My mind immediately raced with possibilities. Was it one of Vale's men? One of Rellik's? Or was it something else entirely? Another threat?

My hand hovered near the curtain, debating whether to call for John or keep watching. But before I could decide, the door creaked open behind me.

"Tori."

I spun around so fast my hair landed right back in my face.

"John?" I mumbled while removing the strands behind my ear. "Did you, did you find them?"

He closed the door behind him, and the look in his eyes made my knees go weak. I was ready to fall to my knees, to die at that very moment.

But then.

I heard it

"They're both alive."

For a second, I thought I misheard him.

"What?"

He nodded, breathing out.

"They're alive. Both of them."

The words hit me like a spear, knocking the breath right out of my lungs. My hand covered my mouth as the tears welled instantly. I didn't even try to stop them.

"How? What? Are you sure? I, we heard the shot."

John's voice was calm, but his eyes still held the weight of chaos.

"It was a soldier. Some punk, no one knew. Honestly, we are not sure what side he represents. He tried to take out Rellik as he and Tino faced off. Tino saw him aim and shoved Rellik out of the way. Took the hit in the shoulder himself."

My mouth dropped open.

"Wait, what. Someone tried to kill my brother, but Vale saved him?"

John nodded.

"Yeah. Took the bullet meant for your brother."

A sob broke in my chest. I turned back toward the window, overwhelmed. The shadow was gone now. Maybe it was never even there. Perhaps it was just my nerves, or maybe it was a warning that tonight had changed everything. I leaned my forehead against the glass, my tears silent but steady. He saved him after everything; he still saved him.

Behind me, John's voice was gentler now.

"They were both pulled out safely. Rellik went quiet after. Said nothing. Just left with his men. Tino headed out, too. Not sure where they took him."

I physically dropped back into the chair, my head melting into my palm, feeling like the room was closing in on me. The weight of both of them surviving pressed hard, heavier than anything I have ever felt before. Both survived. This is what I wanted. But yet, both were hurt. And who was the guy who took the shot?

"John, who was the kid. Did they get him?" I asked.

John looked at me, wishing he had the correct answer,

"No, just vanished. I heard both sides are on a manhunt as we speak."

My mind fractured into two halves, each screaming for a different loyalty.

Rellik.

The brother who built walls around me, every which way I moved. The man created rules to keep me in check. The man who carried our father's legacy was fierce, unyielding, and sometimes cruel. But as he told me, he continued this for me, for us. He was my family, blood thicker than water, the man I was supposed to trust above all else. The man that I would want to walk me down the aisle one day.

And then there was Valentino.

The ghost from my past, the man who made every

ounce of me burn, the man I thought was gone forever. The man who disappeared without a word then returned without skipping a beat. The one who saved my brother's life even as he tore mine apart.

I couldn't breathe through the confusion.

Images flashed Rellik's sharp jaw set in anger, the last time we spoke, the way he held me back when I tried to break free. His hands that could bruise, but also protect.

Then Vale's fingers brushing my hair, the weight of his gaze when he called me my Queen, the bullet that found his shoulder instead of my brother's heart.

How could I choose between the man who imprisoned me and the one who freed me, only to wound me once again?

A storm raged inside my mind, my body, a war without end.

I swallowed hard, my throat numbed. Somewhere in the distance, John's voice echoed softly, a reminder that I wasn't alone, that I had to hold myself together.

But how?

How do you pick sides when your heart is torn in two?

I heard the gate open; I quickly went to the window to see if it was Rellik coming home. But it wasn't him. The car looked familiar. It was one of the matte-muscle cars that helped Rebecca and me during the chase. I saw John head out to the car; he went to the driver's side as they rolled down the window. I couldn't tell who was driving. As minutes passed, John looked up at me, staring at the window. I looked back at him in desperation. The car left right after, and John returned to the house.

John returned seconds later, phone in hand, face tighter than before.

"Well?" I asked, standing too quickly.

"Did they say anything?"

He shook his head.

"No."

I didn't believe him.

Why would he even allow any King on Killer property?

"And Rellik?" I questioned.

"Still no word from Rellik. Our men pulled him out fast and disappeared into one of the protective routes. No one's talking. Even if I tried to go looking, there are too many routes to go through. We have these in place for a reason."

"So, we are back to square one; we know nothing about either one?" My voice cracked.

"I think neither one wants to be found. Not yet."

I turned away, my fists clenched at my sides. That was so like them. To vanish. To demand loyalty while giving nothing in return. They were more alike than they wanted to admit.

John hesitated. "There's something else. One of the soldiers who saw the aftermath said Rellik didn't even look at Tino after it happened, just walked away. Didn't speak. Didn't even check on him."

Of course, he didn't.

That felt like Rellik, too.

Still, the words hit harder than I expected. My brother, who would've died if not for Vale, still refused to see that he really is the same boy, the guy who was like a brother to him.

I pressed my palms against my temples, the pressure building behind my eyes. Every second that passed twisted the knot in my chest tighter. The silence from Rellik wasn't just unsettling. It felt deliberate. Like he wanted me to suffer the weight of the choice he knew I'd have to make.

And beneath it all, I could feel the shift in the air like something had snapped between them. Something I might never be able to fix.

And how could Vale not be trying to reach me? Unless. Unless the bullet wound was worse than they are saying.

I sat down again, but not in panic this time, in paralysis. The kind where you're still actually breathing, but nothing else is moving, just like a dream paralysis. I went into shock.

So much time had passed since the gunshot. The sun was already out, and still no word. My thoughts spun in useless circles. No amount of logic could untangle what I felt. There were no instructions on what to do next for this kind of heartbreak. No rulebook for when your brother becomes your captor and your first love shows up six years later.

 I slowly started to move.

First my fingers, then my head just slightly.

I leaned my head back and closed my eyes.

Memories of my brother coming to.

He was sixteen, and I was fourteen. A boy already pretending to be a man. Papi was out on business, and the school dance was coming up. He drove me to the mall and helped me pick out a dress. Something that other girls were doing with their mothers, I was doing with my big brother. He even bought it.

"You never have to feel alone, he said with a small smile. "Never. Not while I am still breathing." That version of him still lived somewhere inside me. The protector, the sweetheart. The boy who stepped in when I always needed him the most.

Then a memory of Valentino.

We were lying on the rooftop of his house late one night. The stars were faint, the air thick with summer. I remember tracing patterns over his ribs, his voice barely louder than the wind.

"If this life ever tears us apart," he whispered, "I'll

still find a way to love you. Even if I have to love you from a distance."

I didn't answer right away. I just curled closer to Vale, pretending the world below couldn't touch us.

But even then, I felt his fear. He needed to protect me from something he wouldn't name.

And even now, I couldn't forget that night.

The way he held me was like I was the last good thing in his world.

And now here I was, trapped between them.

One built the walls that kept me in.

The other taught me what it felt like to want out.

Rellik had always demanded loyalty since he took Papi's place. He loved me in silence, in control, in orders I never got to question.

Vale loved me in chaos. In fire. In stolen hours and broken promises, but he'd also loved me when no one else dared to.

My body leaned toward one.

My blood whispered the other's name.

I opened my eyes and fought back the sting. There was no correct answer. Only risk. Only ruin.

But I couldn't stay suspended in this in-between. I had to choose where to go, who to look for, and who to find before the guilt swallowed me whole.

I stood slowly, like my body had made the decision before my mind and heart could collaborate.

I could keep sitting here, drowning in what-ifs. I could wait for John to come in and tell me he had heard from Rellik or another King to arrive with a message that Vale was gone.

But waiting hadn't saved anyone tonight. Waiting hadn't stopped the blood or the gunfire or the truth from tearing through everything I thought I knew.

And maybe this wasn't about choosing sides.

Maybe it was about choosing myself for once.

Valentino had disappeared once, but he came back. Not just for me, for all of it. He no longer wanted to be bound to the South Side. He no longer wanted to rule alone. Deep down, I think he wanted to run Gravenport with his Queen by his side.

And tonight, he stepped in front of a bullet meant for my brother.

That meant something.

I asked him not to pull the trigger if he had the choice. And instead, he went a step further to prove his love, his love for me.

Even if I didn't know what came next, even if it broke everything else. I owed him more than silence. I owed us a conversation that wasn't shaped by grief or fear or someone else's rules.

I went out to the hall. No soldiers, no noise. Nothing.

I looked at John, who stood near the door like he already knew.

"You're going to him, aren't you?" he asked softly, eyes not making contact.

I nodded. "Yes. I have to, I need to."

He didn't argue. Just walked me to the front door.

The afternoon air hit me like truth, cold, honest, unavoidable.

My heart pounded louder with every step.

I was still scared. Still unsure. But I was done letting fear choose for me.

I was headed to find Valentino.

And maybe I didn't know what I'd find when I got there, but I knew what I was leaving behind.

The car ride was quiet.

The driver who had waited all this time did not ask me one question. The silence between us wasn't awkward; it was heavy, but necessary, like the kind that comes after a funeral. Something had ended. Something I wouldn't get back.

Outside the window, Gravenport faded fast, empty streets, flickering traffic lights, the eerie calm after violence. I watched the city breathe, watched the stillness press against the glass like a ghost.

Every few seconds, I almost told him to turn around.

To find Rellik instead.

I wanted to make sure my brother was okay.

To fix what might already be broken beyond repair.

But I didn't.

Because my heart had already made the decision, and I was tired of second-guessing myself about where I belonged. Deep down, I hope Rellik will understand.

The driver pulled to a stop in front of the beach house, that's the only place I thought Valentino might go, to the place he thought I was still at.

I could see lights on the inside. Movement through the curtain. A shape, his shape shifting in the shadows.

I hesitated at the door, just for a moment.

Then I got out.

The sand sifted through the air as I stepped. And every step I took toward that door felt like it was stitched in something permanent.

Not an ending. Not yet.

But something close.

CHAPTER 11

The moment I stepped back into the house, Vale's eyes snapped to me.

Without a word, he crossed the space in two long strides and pulled me into a fierce embrace. His arms locked around me like he was afraid I might slip through his fingers again.

The noise from the others, the chatter, the footsteps faded into nothing as he tightened his hold.

"Victoria, where were you? Why didn't you answer my calls?" he whispered against my hair, voice rough with emotion. "God, I thought maybe I was going to have to …"

Before I could say anything, his hand shot out to the door, where a few men lingered in the hall, waiting for orders.

"Get out," he barked. "Now. Leave us."

Footsteps hurried away. The door clicked shut with a finality that echoed in the silence.

Vale took a step back just enough to look at me, his jaw clenched tight.

"Do you know how worried I've been?" His voice cracked, anger and fear tangled in every word. "You left. Disappeared. I thought…"

"I'm sorry," I whispered, my voice barely steady. "I

had to."

My eyes wandered to his shoulder.

"Are you hurt? "I stammered, reaching for the bandage.

He shook his head, frustration burning through his eyes. "I'll live. Victoria, you can't just go back to Gravenport, especially by yourself. Not when everything's falling apart."

But then his gaze softened, the anger melting into something raw and honest.

"You could have been taken, again. You were safe here."

I swallowed the lump in my throat. Valentino's hands lingered on my arms, grounding me, pulling me back from the edge I hadn't even realized I was standing on.

"I needed to try," I said, my voice trembling. "To save you. To save my brother, to save you both. I didn't want to be the reason I lost either one of you."

His glare gradually shifts into something closer to concern, as if he were bracing himself for what I might say next.

 "You may have saved him," my voice gentler now. "And for that, my love for you only grows stronger. But I can't promise Rellik will see it that way."

He took in a deep breath, as if every word had affected him.

"These past few days." I pause, trying to make sure he understands what I am going through. "They've taken everything from me, my body, my heart, my soul."

He searched my face, torn between the need to fight for me and the need to shield me from the pain he knew was coming.

The atmosphere was different now.

Before, when we felt safe, it had been calm. Now, with the future pressing down on us, it was tense. The kind of quiet that came before something broke.

I heard the waves through the creaks in the door and just let Vale hold me for a few minutes, letting the silence say what words couldn't.

Then he shifted.

"Sit down," he said gently. "I need you to understand something."

He knelt next to me, lowering himself until we were eye level.

This was serious.

"Six years ago," he began, "I knew you were the one—the one I loved and wanted to be with forever. And even though your brother, fuck, even the universe tried to keep us apart, you found me. You came back into my life and filled a hole that was destroying me without you."

He reached for my hand, gripping it tightly.

"Victoria Marcano, like I told you the night you came back, I will give it all up to be with you. The title. The territory. Everything. So, if you're willing, let's go. Leave Gravenport behind. Let your brother have the city. Let's start over."

His eyes held me captive, dark, vulnerable, searching.

I wanted to look away.

I wanted to throw myself into his arms.

But I froze.

"Deep down, I always knew how this would end," he said, voice low. "With you and me leaving Gravenport. But this has to be your choice."

I swallowed hard. My throat suddenly went dry.

I'd known he cared. But this, this felt like a confession. A breaking down of walls I'd never been allowed to see.

Was he really willing to give up everything for me?

The Title.

The Territory.

The Power.

The South Side.

I bit my lip, heart pounding. That word "future" sounded so unfamiliar amid the chaos around us. But it sparked something inside me, a flicker of hope

I thought I'd buried.

"Why now?" I asked, with a hint of a whisper.

"Because I can't keep pretending this is just about the war," he said. "It's never been about that. It's you, it always has and always will be about you."

I felt my defenses crumbling, but fear still wrapped around my heart like bandages holding it in one piece.

Could I trust him?

Could I trust myself?

"You're willing to give it all up?" I asked, voice slightly shaky. "For me?"

His hand brushed against mine, hesitant, but sure.

"Everything," he whispered. "I will give up everything to have your trust. Your heart. I want to build a life where you're not running, not hiding, where you can breathe without looking over your shoulder every second. Where the panic attacks stop, for good."

Before I knew it, a tear slipped down my cheek, ever so softly.

All I'd ever wanted was to feel safe. To be seen. To be loved. But that desire was tangled in a web of years of silence, betrayal, and the ache of unanswered questions.

I sat there next to him silently, just for a moment, the weight of unspoken fears thickening the air. I heard my heartbeat before I heard my voice.

"Okay," I said finally, my smile trembling but real. "Okay."

But the words that followed shattered that peaceful moment.

"Before I leave, before we move forward, I need to say goodbye to my brother."

Vale's entire body stiffened. His eyes narrowed, and his hand slipped from mine. "Victoria," he said, voice low. "You know you have to do this on your own. If I see him, I don't know if I can stop myself. We are still at war."

"I know," I said. "But I can't just walk away without seeing Rellik one last time. Not like this."

He leaned back in the chair, dragging his hand through his hair, the tension crawling up his arms.

"He's not going to just give you a hug and wave you off," he muttered. "You know that, right?"

"I'm not expecting that," I said, voice tightening. "I'm expecting..."

I stopped myself.

Because the truth was, I wasn't going just to say goodbye. I needed answers. Needed to face Rellik one last time to truly see if he could just let me go and be happy for me.

But I couldn't tell Vale that.

If he knew what I was planning, he'd stop me.

He studied me for a long moment, jaw clenched. Then he nodded.

"If you really want to do this, go in the morning. I'll stay back. I'll wait for you to return, so we can start fresh."

I nodded, swallowing as if I had molasses in my mouth. This was the moment before the storm.

The rest of the night passed with us planning. We mapped out the route. Identified safe houses. Outlined contingencies for every scenario, on what to do if Rellik refused to let me leave, if things escalated, and if I didn't come back.

Vale was calm through it all. Fierce and grounded. Loyal in a way that both soothed me and made my heart ache.

Every time I looked at him, I saw the man who had risked everything to be beside me again.

And I saw a man I wasn't sure I deserved.

By the time dawn crept through the cracked blinds, I felt fragile but determined.

I had a plan.

A confession.

A goodbye to make.

And the weight of it all threatened to crush me before I even left the room.

I kissed Valentino, slow and lingering, memorizing the heat of his skin and the quiet way his breath stilled when he held me. Then I slipped out, back toward the city.

My thoughts were all over the place on the ride back to the North Side. But there was no changing my mind. I had to do this.

Valentino arranged for a quiet surveillance crew to make sure he knew where Rellik was, so I wasn't going around the city looking for him. Just one stop, that's all I needed. That gave me some relief.

Still, dread curled in my stomach.

The ride over felt like an eternity, but finally, I was there.

The moment I got out of the car, panic set in.

Each step down the hall felt like walking through water, slow and heavy, the pressure of what was coming, building with every second.

Butterflies churned violently in my gut, then turned into cold sweats.

I could do this. I had to do this.

I reached the office door. My hand hesitated on the knob, the speech I'd rehearsed in the car suddenly vanishing from my mind.

I didn't knock.

I walked in.

Rellik sat at his desk, cigarette burning low in the ashtray. He looked up slowly, eyes narrowing the moment he saw me.

Before I could speak, before I could say how relieved I was that he was alive, he cut me off.

"You've got some nerve walking in here," he said coldly. "After everything."

I shut the door behind me, ignoring the dryness in my throat.

"What do you mean, after everything? It doesn't matter. I'm not here to fight. I just came to say goodbye."

That stopped him. He stood up fast, too fast, his whole body going rigid.

"Goodbye?" His voice turned sharp, dangerous. "To whom?"

"To you. Who else?"

The silence that followed was thick and heavy. Rellik's jaw clenched, that vein in his neck twitching like a trigger.

"You're not going anywhere, Tori."

"I forbid it."

"Yes. I am," I said calmly, though my pulse was racing. "You forbid it? I'm not fifteen, bro."

I took a breath, steadying myself.

"Look, I love you. I always will. But I came to say goodbye before Valentino, and I leave the city."

That was it, a match to gasoline.

Rellik lunged around his desk, sending his chair spinning. Fury twisted across his face.

"You're leaving with Tino?" he barked. "The fuck you are*!* After everything I've done to protect you from him?"

My chest tightened. "Protect me from what? Him loving me?"

His lip curled, disgusted. "I kept you safe. I kept you alive. He doesn't care about you, Tori. You think he loves you, but you don't know what he's done."

"I know enough," I said, standing my ground. "And whatever it is, it doesn't matter. Nothing that Valentino could've done would change my mind."

That did it.

That woke the bear.

Rellik roared and punched the wall behind him, his fist slamming through the plaster. The sound cracked through the room like thunder. I half-expected his men to burst in.

"It doesn't matter?" he shouted. "Nothing could change your mind?"

His chest heaved.

"Papi's death doesn't matter, huh?"

My breath hitched.

"What does Papi have to do with...?" I barely got the words out.

Rellik stared at me, his eyes dark and unreadable, like part of him still wanted to protect the little girl he raised. But the fury won.

"He was your hero. And when you learn how he died, who took him from you. You won't just lose that goodness in your heart, you'll lose yourself." His voice was low, cutting deep with every word.

"How can you not put the fucking pieces together, Tori? Your precious King. He chuckled sarcastically. "Let me tell you, baby sis.

It was

Vale.

Fucking.

Tino.

He killed Papi."

He said it slowly, deliberately.

"He pulled the trigger. He's the reason he's dead."

The room spun. I froze. Couldn't breathe.

"You're lying. You asshole, why are you lying?"

"I wish I were." His voice dropped, rage simmering beneath the surface.

"You want details? Fine. But don't say I didn't warn you, your whole world's about to crumble."

He paced once, then locked eyes with me.

"Do you remember the night Papi and I were arguing?"

"Yes," I whispered.

"Because there was a run that needed to be made," he continued, voice tight with bitterness. "The runner never showed, so I told him I'd do it. He called me a child, said I'd just fuck it up, and decided to go himself. I was twenty. A man, not a child. But he chose to go."

I shook my head. "That has nothing to do with Vale."

"Just wait," Rellik snapped. "I'm not done."

He swallowed hard, forcing himself on.

"You remember the crash, the car that slammed into the driveway? I thought we were under attack. I grabbed you, locked you in the closet, and told one of Papi's men to secure the door. When I ran outside, Papi was in the passenger seat, bleeding from a bullet wound to the chest, unconscious. The driver's side, empty. John was down the street, bleeding from his face and the back of his head, out cold. Papi died in my arms. Then I went back to you, still covered in his blood, hugged you tight, and promised to protect you always. Because I knew it was just the two of us now. I had to take care of us."

I stood frozen, taking it all in, the weight of the

memories hitting me like a tidal wave. New information about that night overwhelmed me with emotions. Tears traced slow paths down my face.

"So that's why John never wanted to talk about his scar," I whispered. "It did involve that night."

Rellik nodded grimly.

"John was in the hospital for three weeks. I took over the Killers, turned over every rock, trying to find out what happened, what went wrong."

I interrupted softly, "I remember those weeks you were in and out, keeping me far from it. Then, Vale lost his mom. And then..."

"Oh, I know what you're thinking," he said sharply. "But let me finish."

"That Saturday, the 14th," he said, voice heavy. "John woke up. I was there. He told me who was driving the car. Who decked him when he tried to stop them?"

He paused, letting the words settle.

"It was Tino."

"That doesn't mean he killed..." I started.

"I'm not done!" Rellik snapped, eyes blazing. "Just like you, to defend him before you know the whole story."

I swallowed hard, fear clawing its way up my throat, bracing myself for what was coming next.

"That night, before I could even look for him, he showed up at the office. He came for one reason, something to do with you. But before he could say more, I had John, freshly out of the hospital, step behind him, blocking the exit.

"Tori, I looked him in the eye and asked, 'Were you there? Did you drive the car?'"

"I didn't think he shot Papi. I thought he just knew who did. But you know what happened next. The man I considered my brother dropped to his knees. He confessed he was the one who pulled the fucking trigger."

I gasped.

"No!"

"Oh, yes, baby sis," Rellik said.

"He said it was an accident. Wouldn't give me all the details. But he swore on his mother's grave that it was a deal gone wrong."

I shook my head, backing away.

"No. No, Valentino wouldn't."

"He did." Rellik's voice snapped.

"And I was the one who cleaned up the mess. I buried the truth for you. So, you wouldn't grow up hating the boy you loved, blaming yourself, broken forever."

"So, the man I once called my brother wouldn't be buried in the dirt next to his mother."

He swallowed hard, pain flickering behind his eyes.

"I gave him a choice. To leave the North Side. Leave you. Never come back into our lives. And I would turn the other way."

"He was a brother to me. Was I supposed to kill him? I couldn't pull the trigger even though every ounce of me wanted to avenge Papi. I kept seeing you heartbroken."

"So, John and I decided to keep it buried. Knowing the risk if The Killers ever found out. But I was the Leader now, I would take the fall."

My heart cracked wide open.

"Why didn't you tell me?"

"Because I knew it would destroy you," he said, softer now.

"Papi was your whole life. You were already broken. Rebecca tried to help, but nobody could get through to you, not really."

"And recently?" I asked, voice barely steady.

"Because I didn't want you running back to him like this," Rellik said.

"You think he stayed close for you? I'm telling you now, he didn't stay close for fucking love, Tori. It's guilt. It's him trying to feel better about something he caused."

Tears blurred my vision, but I blinked them away.

I didn't know what hurt more, what Rellik had said, or that some part of me believed him.

"Did you ever think," I whispered, "that I had a right to know? That I could've made my own choices?"

"You were barely eighteen," he said. "Broken. And he left you without a word. That should've been enough."

I turned toward the door, hands shaking.

"I'm going to him. I need to hear this from him."

Rellik's voice dropped low, dangerous.

"Tori, I swear to God if you go to him, even after knowing the truth, you're dead to me. You hear me?"

I paused.

"I love you, brother," I said quietly.

"But I need to hear it from him. I need him to tell me if he killed Papi."

And then I opened the door and walked out.

I didn't slam it.

I didn't scream.

I didn't cry or collapse like I thought I might if the truth ever came out.

Instead, I walked.

Slow.

Empty.

Careful, like if I moved too fast, I'd fall apart right there in the hallway.

The air outside hit my face like a slap, calm, sharp, and utterly unaware that my entire world had just shattered down the middle.

He pulled the trigger.

The words echoed louder with every step I took.

They no longer sounded like Rellik's.

They sounded like my own voice, taunting me, daring me to deny what I knew now.

I kept walking.

Past the front gate.

I saw John. His eyes locked onto mine for a moment before dropping, his hand brushing gently over the scar on his face.

It was as if he knew.

I thought, this can't be true.

My stomach churned.

It all made sense now why John never helped me, why Rellik set those rules once Vale formed the South Side Kings.

Everything was unraveling.

I passed the men who gave me wary glances, but

they didn't stop me.

My fingers curled tightly around the strap of my bag, trying to keep them from shaking.

I had no destination, only a certainty.

I needed to see him.

I needed his eyes on mine.

I needed to hear him say it.

I didn't want comfort.

I didn't want apologies.

I wanted the truth. Vale's truth.

Because if he looked me in the eye and confirmed it, if he said the words without fear or hesitation, then whatever we had left would shatter for good.

Or maybe, it already had.

I tried to remember that night.

The one I never questioned.

The silence in Rellik's voice.

The funeral.

The way no one looked me in the eye for days.

Was it all a lie?

I wiped my face, surprised to find tears there, without knowing when they started.

Before I headed back to the beach house, I needed to go home.

Needed to gather my thoughts. Maybe even my things.

I arrived at my place.

Each step felt heavier than the last as I approached the door.

I pushed it open.

And stepped inside.

CHAPTER 12

The front door clicked shut behind me like a verdict.

Silence wrapped itself around the house like a weighted blanket, thick and calming.

But I was suffocating.

Suffocating in my thoughts.

My fears.

The truths.

The faint hum of the refrigerator grounded me back to reality.

I dropped my keys into the bowl by the door, fingers numb, heart heavier.

Rellik's voice echoed in my mind, again and again.

Tori, if you go to him after everything you know, you're dead to me.

Dead.

Just like Papi.

What he didn't realize was that whatever hope and love I had this morning, it was already gone.

I felt hollow.

Dead inside.

I paced the small living room, dragging my bare feet across the hardwood floor.

That same floor Rellik had polished countless times, wanting to make sure that if I were going to live here, it would be perfect.

I saw him then, leaning against the doorframe, arms crossed, those sharp eyes that never missed a thing.

He was just like Papi.

"Family is everything, Victoria," my dad used to say when we were little.

I remembered the night he held me and told me again how family was everything, the weight of his words imprinting in my core memories.

"Sometimes the world is cruel, but blood, blood is forever."

If only he'd known he wouldn't be here.

That Rellik and I would be alone.

I sank into the worn leather couch, its cold surface pressing against my skin.

My mind drifted back to one summer afternoon, years ago.

Papi had taken me fishing at the lake, just the two of us.

The sun had kissed my skin, the world so quiet except for the soft crunch of sunflower seeds between his teeth.

I was struggling to bait my hook, fumbling clumsily, close to tears. He crouched beside me and adjusted my baseball cap.

"Hey, it's okay to mess up sometimes," Papi said, voice soft.

"You don't have to be perfect, my little Victoria. Just don't give up."

I'd looked up at him, wide-eyed, trying so hard to believe him.

"What if I fail?"

He smiled.

The kind of smile that made you feel like your father could stop time.

"Then you get up and try again. Falling down is just part of learning how to stand on your own."

That moment was so small.

So simple.

But it was everything.

And now, I clung to it like a lifeline, something to hold on to while everything else fell apart.

My phone sat in my hand, freshly charged after days

without it.

I finally had it back.

I thought about calling Rellik to hear his voice, to feel even the faintest connection to the brother I used to know.

But what if the voice on the other end was cold?

Or worse, what if there were no words at all?

My thumb hovered over his name in my contacts.

I thought of his rage.

The way his eyes hardened when I defied him.

The way his hand struck my face, once, but hard enough to crack something that might never heal.

No.

I let the phone fall onto the counter and pressed my hands down, shifting my weight forward. A scream tore from my throat, sharp, siren-like. I was mad. Hurt. Trembling.

I needed a shower. I needed to wash off the hate and devastation. I needed to cry.

The water hit my skin like fire, cleansing away yesterday's tears but not the ache in my chest. In the steam, his face haunted me. Vale's smile. The way his eyes locked in with mine as if I were the only thing in the world.

The way he whispered, "Tell me you don't believe

that we all fall down sometimes."

I clung to that memory like a lifeline, even if the truth behind it might be the secret that finally breaks us.

Afterward, I stepped out and wrapped a towel around myself. I pulled clothes from the closet, my mind scattered. I still didn't know what I planned to do next. But just in case, I packed a small bag. Essentials. And something meaningful.

Jeans. A hoodie. My old perfume bottle was tucked into the side pocket. A few things from the bathroom. A necklace from the jewelry box.

Then I saw it.

Lying on the bed was a folded photograph, three smiles frozen in time.

Me. Rellik. Vale.

The past felt like a ghost, hovering just out of reach.

I sat on the edge of the bed, tracing the edges of the photo with trembling fingers.

What am I running toward?

What am I leaving behind?

The room around me suddenly felt too small. Shifting it in all directions. Too full of memories I hadn't made peace with. I pressed the photo to my chest and breathed in the echoes of better days before the secrets, before the lies, before everything splintered.

A soft knock made me jump.

But it was only the wind.

Or maybe just my heart pounding in the quiet.

I slipped the photo into my bag and zipped it closed, each tooth of the zipper like a reluctant goodbye.

Before I left, I glanced around the apartment one last time, soaking it all in.

Then I whispered to the empty room, "I don't want to be broken anymore."

The engine hummed beneath me as the Northside was behind me. The road stretched ahead, glowing, unfamiliar to me. I gripped the steering wheel tighter, but my thoughts drifted far behind me, tangled in what-ifs and memories.

What would I even say to him?

Do I hug him? Kiss him?

Could I even look at him?

Was Rellik right?

Had Vale come back because of guilt?

The thought made my chest clench.

I ran my fingers through my hair and glanced at the passenger seat. My bag sat there, silent and heavy, like the secret I still carried.

I didn't know whether to stay or leave, or whether I was ready to forgive or to say goodbye for good. If I were chasing answers or just chasing ghosts.

The ocean air drifted through the cracked window, salty and sharp. I was close now.

The beach house loomed in the distance, where so many of our memories had lived. And maybe where they'd come to die.

My phone buzzed again. I didn't look.

Not yet.

Maybe it was Rellik. Maybe Vale. Maybe more pain waiting to be read.

I needed silence.

I needed this.

I pulled up in front of the beach house. The wind howled across the sand as I stepped out, gravel crunching under my shoes.

I stared at the front door.

My feet felt like cement. Heavy. Unmoving.

What was I so afraid of?

I walked in, and my eyes immediately locked with his. I started to cry.

Vale rushed toward me.

I put out a hand to stop him.

"**Tino**, don't you dare," I said.

He froze not because of the tears or even the gesture, but because I called him *Tino*.

I'd only ever used that name once before. I thought it would stop him and Rellik from arguing.

"He told you, didn't he?" he asked, guilt thick in his voice.

My eyes filled again. I took a shaky breath and looked Vale straight in the face.

"Is it true?" I asked, my heart barely holding together.

"Victoria…"

But before he could say anything more, the door flew open.

Vale instinctively stepped in front of me, shielding me.

We both turned.

Frozen.

It was Rellik. He must've followed me.

"Go ahead, Tino," Rellik said, voice sharp, almost reprimanding. "Answer her question."

"Get out," Vale snapped.

"No," Rellik barked back. "I think Victoria deserves to hear the truth. And so, do I. Even when you confessed, you refused to tell me everything. We deserve to know the whole fucking truth."

I moved toward Rellik and grabbed his arm. My voice cracked.

"Tell me, Valentino, did you kill Papi?"

"Yes," he said. The word came out broken.

My knees buckled. Rellik caught me before I could fall, holding me upright with both arms. My body was ice, trembling.

"Why?" I stammered.

"It's not like that. Please let me explain." Vale started pacing, raking a hand through his hair. "My mother was sick. Cancer. The bills were endless. The doctors told us there was nothing else they could do unless we paid upfront. I was desperate."

"You killed our father for money?" Rellik spat.

"No. Fuck no." Vale exhaled sharply, shaking his head. "That wasn't the plan."

"Then what?" I whispered. I didn't even recognize my voice.

Vale looked at me, wrecked. "One night after I left your house, some guy stopped me. He was definitely one of your father's men. Said he had a job, told me the time, and the location of a run. All I had to do was disrupt it. Scare off the runner. He said he'd give me a gun with blanks to make sure the deal didn't happen. If I did, they'd pay me $50K."

Rellik and I exchanged the smallest glance just enough to confirm we were both processing the same thing.

He guided me gently to the couch, knowing I couldn't stay standing. He stayed behind me, his hands on my shoulders. I reached up and gripped one of them with my right hand, grounding myself. I leaned my head slightly back against him.

"Go on," Rellik said tightly.

"I took the deal."

I gasped.

"Victoria," Vale said. "You need to understand I was desperate. My mother was dying. I was only supposed to scare him. It was supposed to be a fucking runner. But it wasn't. When I approached the guy from behind, gun out, he turned and grabbed it. It went off. And it wasn't until the shot was fired that I realized it wasn't blanks. And it wasn't just some foot soldier. It was your dad. Yours and Rellik's."

Tears streamed down my face. I looked at Rellik. He slid his sunglasses on like a shield, but I knew him too well. Hearing the details of how Papi died, it was hitting him, too.

"I grabbed him right away," Vale continued. "I placed him in the passenger seat and drove straight to your house. I tried to stop the bleeding with one hand and steer with the other. I crashed into your driveway. I panicked. I knew the crash would bring people out. I was afraid, afraid of losing you. Of losing you both. So, I ran."

His voice cracked.

"I heard Rellik shouting to guard you in the closet. I knew I couldn't get to you. That's when John saw me and told me not to move. So, I decked him. Right in the eye. He hit the concrete so hard that he stayed down. I ran home. Ashamed. I didn't even collect the money. And weeks later, my mother was gone."

He swallowed hard.

"When I finally wanted to move on with you, I... I went to Rellik to tell him about us. But John was there. And, well, you know the rest."

I just sat there. Numb. Swallowed by the weight of it all.

Before I could say another word, I heard it.

Crack!

Rellik slammed a punch into Vale's ribs.

"You betrayed our family for money!" he spat, as if the words burned his tongue. "You could have come to me!"

I jumped up as Rellik pulled back for another hit, but Vale tackled him. They crashed through the table, splinters flying. No soldiers. No guards. Just the two of them, brother against brother.

I couldn't breathe.

"Tino, stop! Rellik, please, stop! *Por favor*!" I screamed.

But they didn't. They didn't even hear me.

So, I did the only thing I could.

I left.

I needed to clear my head. Finally, knowing the truth was eating me alive. I got in my car and drove off. In the rearview mirror, I saw Rellik coming out of the house, scanning the street like he was already looking for me.

But what was I supposed to do?

Now that I knew the whole story, what choice did I really have? He didn't mean to do it. It wasn't planned. He didn't realize until it was too late. But still, he kept it from me for years. And then he stood beside me, knowing I was shattered, knowing he was the reason.

I let out a shaky breath, then inhaled slowly and steadily. My lungs expanded, chest rising as I started counting inside my head.

"One, two, three, four, five, six, seven..."

And finally, "eight."

I exhaled. My shoulders dropped with the breath. I just needed to breathe, to slow the chaos in my mind.

Okay. Just a little more time.

I kept driving. The sky was softening with the last rays of the sun, painted in streaks of orange and lavender. Peaceful. Quiet.

Then, in the distance, I saw headlights flash at me

once, then twice, giving me a warning.

I slowed instinctively.

That's when I saw it, just around the bend.

A car. Broken down.

My chest constricted.

Rebecca's car.

I grabbed my phone and pushed her icon on my home screen, but it went straight to voicemail. I hit the emergency button on my dashboard and eased to the side of the road.

Her front tire was missing.

"Shit," I whispered, stepping out. "Did she have a blowout? Why didn't she call me?"

But as I got closer, something felt off. Way off.

The front driver's side tire wasn't just gone; it's as if it never happened. There were no fragments, no signs of a blowout. The rim was carved raw from being dragged across the pavement. It looked like someone had ripped it off on purpose.

My pulse spiked.

I called out her name. "Rebecca?"

No answer.

I turned to run back to my car, fumbling for my keys.

I'd left my phone inside.

The wind picked up, cold, sharp, biting at my skin. I pressed the unlock button on my car remote. The beep echoed into the emptiness around me.

I exhaled and reached for the handle.

Then I heard it.

A sound. Behind me.

I froze.

Before I could turn, hands grabbed me. Cold, firm, and merciless.

I screamed, but it was muffled; something pressed over my mouth. I dropped my keys. I kicked, flailed anything.

But it was already dark.

There were no headlights. No cars. No help.

It was a trap.

And I walked straight into it.

This can't be happening…

Not now.

Not like this.

Valentino's POV

Rellik had left after Victoria.

Now that she knows the truth, have I lost her forever?

Rage and guilt surged through my veins like wildfire. The air was thick, just like the tension that lingered after Rellik's departure. I reached for my phone to call her.

But headlights cut through the night. A car skidded to a stop outside, horn blaring in panic.

I stepped out into the moonlight, waves crashing against the shore in the distance. One of my soldiers jumped out, breathless, eyes wide.

"King Vale," he gasped. "The Queen, her car."

He swallowed, voice rough. "It's abandoned. The keys were on the street by the driver's side. Her phone was still on the passenger seat. The window's cracked just slightly as if she was getting air."

My pulse stalled.

"What else was around?" I asked, voice low.

In front of her car was Rebecca's vehicle. The tire is completely gone. She's missing too."

A cold edge sliced through my chest. Someone had taken my Queen, planned it. They knew she'd stop for her best friend. It was a trap.

"Where the hell is she?" I growled, barely containing the violence simmering beneath my skin.

"We searched everything. No footprints. No trails. But just as we were leaving, another SUV pulled up as we left the scene."

I started to pace back and forth. Fully aware that the

other SUV had to be Rellik on his way back to the North Side.

"Get inside. Call everyone. Now. They think they can take her? No. She's mine."

I slammed my fist into the wooden post of the porch.

Within the hour, the beach house was crawling with soldiers. I barked orders as teams moved out.

"I want every inch of the South Side combed. Check the North too, from the Marcanova Estate to the Crown Club. Every alley. Every tunnel. *Entiendes*?"

The men nodded, whispers flying as plans were formed and weapons gathered.

"Make no mistake," I said, voice sharp as steel. "Whoever took her should not have messed with the Kings."

I clenched my jaw, fury burning hot behind my eyes.

"She won't stay missing long. Not if I have anything to say about it."

And whoever had her would regret ever laying a hand on her.

The front door slammed open like a gunshot.

Rellik stormed in, eyes blazing.

"Where the hell is she?" he snapped, voice fire and ice.

I didn't flinch. I was already drowning in my rage,

haunted by the thought of what Victoria must be feeling right now.

"You think I took her?" I snapped. "You left me here to chase after her; now she's gone. Our men screwed up; nobody was watching her. But whoever did this won't be able to hide her for long. Not from me. He thinks I won't find her?" I stepped closer, daring him to challenge me. "She's my Queen. Nobody, and I mean nobody, is going to stop me from getting her back. So, help me or get the fuck out of my way."

Rellik stared at me for one long beat, then shut the door behind him.

He pulled out his phone and started dialing, calling every contact he had.

And just like that, we both knew.

If we wanted her back...

We had no choice but to do this together.

259

www.ingramcontent.com/pod-product-compliance
Lightning Source LLC
Chambersburg PA
CBHW020653120726

47906CB00001B/251